THROUGH THE WINDOW

DENNIS MEREDITH

Disclaimer

This is a work of fiction. Names, characters, places, and incidents are products of the author's imagination or are used fictitiously. Any resemblance to actual persons, living or dead, or real events is purely coincidental.

DEDICATION

This book is for everyone living with mental illness. I hope you find the care, support, and healing you deserve. You are not alone.

Best Wishes

Denis Meredith.

24.7.25

ACKNOWLEDGEMENTS

I'd like to thank Peter Dietrich for his design of the cover, and my wife, Rona, for her patience that she has shown to me.

Table of Contents

Chapter 1
Maria

It was a sweltering day, hot in Ramsgate, and Maria was sitting on her beach chair, relaxing after work at the Springwood Care Home. She always did this when she finished work.

She would go to the beach to her favourite spot, taking her folding chair, which she always kept in her car boot. She always went to the spot away from the rest of the crowd. On some days, the beach at Ramsgate would get very busy. She wanted to be on her own, taking in the sun. She always took a magazine and the morning paper so she could catch up on the news and read her magazine. It was a way for Maria to unwind after working hard for nine hours in the Care Home. She was reasonably well known on the beach because she was a regular visitor, enjoying the sunny days in Ramsgate—a seaside town with plenty of attractions. There was nothing better for Maria to do after work than to relax and chill for the rest of the day.

Maria had a full figure and an average appearance. She had a strong opinion of herself and did not have many friends she could relate to. She kept to herself, except for Pauline at the Care Home. She felt lonely, especially in winter when she couldn't visit the beach and had to return to her well-furnished flat in a block of six. She rarely interacted with her neighbours beyond a simple greeting.

There was an elderly lady who lived in the flat opposite hers. She used to keep an eye out for her, and if she needed anything, Maria would do her shopping. She was happy to do that for her. The lady's name was June. She found it very difficult to walk because she used two walking sticks. Most mornings, Maria would knock on her door to see if she was OK or needed help in any way. June was most appreciative of her help. Sometimes, she would buy Maria some flowers to thank her for keeping an eye on her.

She was quite comfortable financially because she had been left a considerable amount of money by her parents, who came from Italy and used to visit her in England on a number of occasions. Maria looked forward to their visits and loved having her parents stay with her. Although they could not speak English, they still enjoyed visiting the country and going out to dinner with Maria. They had such wonderful times together in England.

Her parents ran a sizeable vineyard in Italy, and it was very well supported by the villagers where they lived. They had several outlets for their wine, and over the years, they ran a successful business and made a considerable amount of money. At that time, the wine they produced was mainly red, and it sold very well. Most of the villagers came to the vineyard to buy wine. People from nearby villages and even all over Italy would also come to purchase it. Tourists on holiday—some from other countries—would visit to taste the wine and buy a few bottles. The wine was distributed across Italy. Some restaurant owners ordered it in bulk for their establishments, and several retail supermarkets also purchased it. During the summer, tourists would advertise special wine-tasting events, and visitors would flock to the vineyard to sample the wine and take a few bottles home in their suitcases.

When Maria was living with them in Italy, she suggested they try to export the wine to Great Britain. She told her father she had heard the British drank a lot of wine. Her father said he didn't want to do that because he wasn't sure if the wine would travel long distances well.

Her mother was a very compassionate lady and was well-liked by the villagers. Every year, they would come and help during the harvest. Maria's mother would put on a party for them all and give them three bottles of wine as a thank-you.

The villagers contributed to the harvest and took part in the celebration that followed. Maria's father said it was one of the highlights of the year. The harvest felt like a holiday for everyone, as they picked grapes and placed them into baskets. Her father would then take the baskets to the sheds for wine production. He had learned about grape mixing for winemaking from his father and grandfather. The family kept their wine recipe a secret.

Unfortunately, a few years ago, Maria's father died from a terminal illness. He had suffered for a long time and underwent treatment for cancer, but it was not successful. One year later, Maria's mother also passed away. She had not done well after her husband died.

Maria considered returning to Italy to take over the business, but she didn't have the will to stay in the house or manage the vineyard. She decided to sell the business to a local consortium for a significant sum of money as a going concern.

Maria came to England five years ago because she wanted to become a State Registered Nurse. She worked at a local general hospital for two years. Then, an opportunity arose for her to become the Head Nurse at Southfields Care Home—a large facility with 120 separate rooms. It was newly built for this purpose. The owners offered Maria a position as a practice nurse connected to the local doctor's practice in the area. Maria thought this was a wonderful opportunity to launch her professional career.

When Maria decided she was going to move to England, her mother was quite upset at the prospect of losing her only daughter. At that time, they had hoped Maria would get married, have children, and take over the family business—but that never happened. Nevertheless, her mother supported her. She used to give Maria an allowance so she could rent a flat in Ramsgate. Maria started work through an agency that paid for her travel to Ramsgate, covered her stay at a local hotel, and reimbursed travel expenses.

Her mother wanted Maria to be independent and not rely on others for accommodation. Eventually, Maria saved up enough money to purchase the flat she now lives in. She bought it from an elderly couple who had passed away; their children put the flat up for sale. When Maria viewed it, she realised it needed a lot of work to make it modern. Money was tight after she paid the deposit, but she had just enough left over to renovate the flat. She was very satisfied once the work was done. Her father had also sent her money to buy furniture and white goods.

Maria never forgot her parents. She had a marvellous upbringing in a loving and caring home. She attended local schools in the village and did very well academically, passing all her exams. She later attended Medical College to train as a State Registered Nurse. She loved being a student at the time and passed with full marks.

Her parents were delighted that she succeeded in becoming a nurse. When she qualified, they came to visit her in Ramsgate. They stayed at a local hotel for four weeks and celebrated her achievement. Her father even helped decorate her flat.

Maria was born and baptised as a Catholic and always kept her faith. She said prayers regularly and attended the local Catholic church in Ramsgate, where her parish priest was Father Benjaman. Maria used to go to the local drop-in at the church and mix with other parishioners. Occasionally, she would light a candle for both her mother and father at Saint Benedict Church. She never liked to miss Sunday Mass, but sometimes she had to work overtime at the Care Home and couldn't attend.

At the Care Home, there were two nurses. The other nurse was Maria's friend, Pauline Watson. She was a State-Enrolled Nurse. Her qualifications weren't the same as Maria's, but she was still a qualified nurse. Between the two of them, they looked after many patients and administered their medication. One thing they both needed in abundance was patience.

The two nurses held weekly meetings to discuss the patients and any concerns. There were fifty staff members working at Southfields. Jobs ranged from cooks to porters, care assistants, nurses, and on-call doctors who worked in shifts around the clock. The Care Home was so full that they could not take in any new clients unless someone left or passed away.

Chapter 2
Care Home

Maria was preparing to go to work in the Care Home on Monday morning, after she had a rest at the weekend, sometimes visiting her favourite beach and doing her shopping for the week. One of her favourite pastimes was watching her favourite soap opera. It was called *My Life in the Country*. This programme is on Monday, Wednesday, and Friday nights.

Although Maria did not realise it herself, she was in love with the main character, Timothy Daly. He was the main character in this soap; the local doctor had his own practice in the village. The soap was centred around the doctor's practice. He was in his late 40s and very well-presented. Maria would never miss an episode on television. Sometimes, if she could not watch it live, she would record the programme so she could never miss an episode. Dr Daly had been in this particular programme for the last five years, and for the last four years, Maria had been watching the programme.

Maria knew that she was falling more and more in love with him. She used to talk quite a lot to the patients she looked after and tried to encourage them to watch the programme. Certain things in the show were in his practice. Doctor Daly visited lots of his patients, and he was based in the village, and he got to know the patients that he served quite well. His patients would love him to come to visit them and sit and talk about different things that were going on in the village.

There was one patient with whom he became very friendly. Sometimes he used to meet her in the local pub called *The Gamekeeper*, and the regulars knew that he had a soft spot for her.

The part that she played was Carol Wantage; she lived in the village in a thatched cottage that she loved.

Some of the residents at the Care Home didn't really like talking about the programme. Maria insisted she would tell them what happened to the doctor in the programmes. She used to fantasise when she was on her own after she watched a particular episode, thinking that one day she would meet Dr Timothy personally. She knows she would never meet him, only by watching the programme on television.

Maria was responsible for many of the patients and clients at the Care Home. Lots of the clients had dementia and could not look after themselves. Hence, they had to have round-the-clock care. She also had some clients for whom she had a lot of feelings; some had been at the Care Home for a long time. Another favourite client was a man called Jimmy West. She would pop in to see him most days and sit with him and talk about his life. She opened the door to his bedroom.

'Jimmy, how are you today?' she asked.

'I am fine, Maria', said Jimmy.

He suffered from respiratory [COPD] complaints. It was very debilitating for him, and he was on several inhalers, which would help him breathe more easily.

Jimmy had difficulty walking; he was bedridden primarily.

Maria asked, 'Would you like me to prop up your pillow, Jimmy?'

'Thank you, yes please', replied Jimmy.

Maria had a look to see if his inhalers were okay and to make sure the inhalers were topped up with medicine.

'They are fine', she said. 'They are OK for you to take'.

Maria was able to write prescriptions if the clients needed any of them when she qualified as an SRN—a State Registered Nurse. She also qualified to prescribe prescriptions.

'I watched my programme last night', she said to Jimmy. 'Dr Jimmy is having a secret affair with one of his patients', she said.

Jimmy answered, 'It is not good, Maria. Can the doctor be struck off?'
Maria chuckled, 'Yes, he can'.

Maria spent half an hour with him because she loved talking about his past. She was very interested in what he had to say regarding his past. Jimmy had reached the age of 96, but he was still able to relate his life story to Maria.

One day, he said to her, 'I will tell you about a special story that happened to me during World War II'.

'That would be nice', Maria answered.

Suddenly, Maria's pager rang, and she told him, 'I have to go, it seems that somebody is calling me'.

Jimmy was upset when Maria left because he loved talking to her. He had grown fond of her. Jimmy was married and had no children. He and his wife, Betty, used to travel round the world exploring different places, so they were quite happy not to have children.

His wife died a few years ago, and he was left on his own. He could not look after himself, and he had to be taken into Southfields Care Home. He was quite happy; he was well looked after and knew he had Maria as a friend.

Jimmy owned a retail shop selling everything electrical, including televisions and washing machines. He employed quite a few people, and it was an extremely popular shop.

He had a manager who used to look after the shop when he went abroad with his wife. The manager had worked for Jimmy for several years, and Jimmy had a lot of trust in him, so he left him to run the business. The business ran smoothly and made lots of profits from the goods that were sold. Jim Robinson was quite upset when he heard that the business was going to be sold to new people. They employed him to continue being the manager of the shop.

Jimmy decided to sell his business and retire. His business was very profitable. Over the years, he became very comfortable and had no money worries. The only problem he had was paying the Care Home, which was quite a considerable amount of money to be looked after. And he used to wonder, if his money ran out, what would happen to him.

Maria always reassured him that he would be safe and well looked after in the Care Home.

'Thank goodness', Jimmy said to himself when Maria told him.

When Maria answered her pager, she had to see another patient who had run out of their medication, and Maria would make sure to write out a prescription for the new medication for the patient.

Chapter 3
Manager

The manager of the Care Home was Mr Ben Hutchinson. He was a kind and caring man. He thought a lot about Maria, and often they would sit in the restroom and have coffee together.

Mr Hutchinson had gone through a traumatic divorce from his wife. He had a flat opposite the Care Home and lived on his own. He didn't mind—he had plenty to occupy his mind, and the Care Home took up a lot of his time.

He had two children from his marriage to his ex-wife, Sheila. They had a boy, who was 11 years old, and a girl, aged 9. He saw them on a regular basis. Sometimes he would take them out for the day, and occasionally they would spend time with him in his flat. The girl's name was Mandy, and the boy's name was Jack.

Mandy used to help tidy her father's flat, and sometimes she would do the washing using the machine. He had to show her how to use it at first, but she soon became quite the expert.

He was very pleased with the way his children were being brought up by his ex-wife. Occasionally, he would take them to the Care Home to meet some of the residents. The residents loved talking to the children and often gave them little treats. Some always looked forward to their visits. If the children didn't come, they would ask the care assistants whether they were visiting soon.

The residents truly enjoyed those moments. The children also loved to hear the residents' stories. On a few occasions, they met Maria, who adored the two of them. At Christmas, Maria always gave them each a gift, which delighted them.

Ben's ex-wife was on speaking terms with Maria. They always got along well. She would stop to say hello whenever she came by, and Ben was pleased that his wife was friendly with the staff.

One day, Ben asked Maria if she would like to go to the theatre with him at the local repertory theatre. He loved drama plays but didn't enjoy going on his own.

'Maria', he said, 'there's a play I'd like to see at the rep this Saturday. I have two tickets. Would you like to come with me?'

Maria answered in a slightly shaky voice, 'Yes, I would love to, Ben'.

He was delighted she accepted the invitation. 'Thank you', he said. 'I'll pick you up at 7 p.m. for a 7.30 p.m. start. I'll meet you outside the Care Home'.

The Care Home was just around the corner—a short walk away.

That Saturday evening, Ben met Maria outside the Care Home at 7 p.m. They walked to the theatre together. Maria thanked him for taking her, noting how kind he was.

'It's my pleasure', he said.

Maria felt quite anxious. This was the first time anyone had shown any personal interest in her. During the performance, she found herself worrying about how the evening might go. *Is this just a one-off date,* she wondered, *or does he want a long-term relationship?*

At the time, Maria had no romantic attachment to Ben beyond friendship and the fact that he was her manager. Still, it was a promising idea, she thought. She began to wonder whether she had done the right thing by accepting his invitation.

After the show, Ben asked, 'Would you like to have a drink before heading home?'

Maria was still a little nervous, but replied, 'I'd love to have one drink with you, Ben. But I must get home soon—I'm going to church tomorrow morning. It's Sunday'.

After they finished their drinks, Ben walked Maria to her flat and wished her goodnight.

Maria was relieved when she got inside. She thought to herself, *Had I been unreasonable or off-putting by not making more of an effort with Ben?*

Chapter 4
Residents

The next morning, Maria couldn't stop thinking about her trip to the theatre with her manager. What would she say to him when she saw him next? She felt embarrassed, having left him at her flat without any explanation.

She arrived at work very early and, first thing in the morning, went in to see Jimmy. She knew she had other residents to attend to who also needed her help. One thing she couldn't quite understand was the policy of referring to the residents as 'clients'. It was a rule set by the manager of the Care Home, based on the fact that residents had to pay a fee to stay there. This was also why she had to explain the terminology to new staff.

Most of them were patients with various types of illnesses. She felt particularly sorry for those suffering from dementia.

When Maria was training to become a nurse, one of the senior professors had told her that to help prevent dementia, people should keep their brains active. He had suggested doing crosswords and jigsaw puzzles, claiming it could help ward off the disease. Maria didn't know if it was scientifically proven, but she tried to keep most of the patients engaged in mentally stimulating activities whenever possible.

Most of the dementia patients were women, which Maria didn't understand at the time. Although there were quite a few men who also suffered from dementia, some of the patients didn't even know who they were—their condition was very advanced. Sometimes, Maria had to care for at least twelve patients a day who needed her help.

One of her favourite patients with the illness was Catherine Wentworth. Maria used to spend a lot of time with her and did her best to support her through the illness. Catherine was in her seventies and had been a primary school teacher, working with children aged five to nine. On several occasions, when Maria was sorting out Catherine's medication, Catherine would mistake her for her mother.

This was a result of her dementia. Maria would go along with it, and although she managed the situation gently, it was sad for her to see how the illness was progressing in someone who had once led such a meaningful life.

Catherine had suffered from dementia for three years. She had lived with her husband, but after a while, he could no longer cope with her condition, and she had to be brought to Southfields Care Home to be looked after. Although it wasn't technically Maria's job to assist her directly, she tried to keep Catherine as bright and cheerful as possible, brushing her hair and making her look presentable.

Sometimes, Catherine was okay. She would have a flashback to her teaching days and tell Maria about the children she used to look after. She even remembered the names of some of her pupils. But those moments were rare, as her mind would often wander. Maria could see that Catherine's time in this world was coming to an end—her condition was deteriorating.

Maria often went to church, lit a candle for her, and prayed, hoping that whatever happened, Catherine would leave this world as peacefully as possible.

Maria had to give a weekly report to the manager, Ben Hutchinson, on the progress of the residents she was caring for. She went to see him and updated him about Catherine's condition.

'Catherine's condition is getting worse', she told Ben.

'I think it's to be expected', he replied. 'I've noticed a deterioration in her. Please do your best for her, and thank you for taking care of her'.

'OK', replied Maria.

With that, she left the office. She didn't say anything to Ben about their date—she was still too embarrassed about having let him go and leaving him at the flat without any explanation.

Chapter 5
Italy

Maria sat down and started writing a report regarding all the clients she had been caring for. When it came down to writing about Catherine's condition her hand started to shake because she was quite upset that she knew Catherine's condition was getting worse but nevertheless she had to finish the report she knew she was going on holiday because she had a letter from the owners back in Italy the letter went on to say that they wanted to make some improvements to the vineyard they have now decided they will start to export the wine they was producing.

Dear Maria,

We request your presence at the vineyard for a special meeting to discuss its further development.

We know you are very busy with your nursing we cannot carry on with the new plans for the vineyard unless you can come to the meeting if it is impossible for you to come, please let us know and I will send you a report with a voting form for you to vote on the new project.

We would like to implement a new venture at the vineyard, as you are a director of this vineyard, your vote is rather important, and we hope that you can attend.

If you can attend, please let us know when you arrive. I will sort out a date for the meeting.

Yours faithfully,
Albert Vannellid
Managing Director and Co-Owner.

Maria was still a shareholder in the vineyard because in the condition of sale, Maria was made a director, and so she had a responsibility to her late mother and father to make sure the vineyard was running successfully.

When she finished the report for the manager, she took it to him and explained that she had to go to Italy and could she take her two-week holiday.

He agreed and he told her she would have to give him a week to find a replacement or a period of two weeks.

'Thank you, Ben', Maria said. 'That's very kind of you, I have no alternative; I have to go'.

'Good luck, Maria'.

Maria decided that she would have to book a flight to Italy and make arrangements.

She was excited that she was going home to Italy, where she would meet all her relations, uncles and aunts, and some of her nieces.

The time came, and it was time for Maria to catch the plane to go to Italy. She made her way to London airport to catch the early morning plane, arriving in Italy at 10:00 PM. She was going to be met by one of her uncles, who was working at the vineyard. The plane took off on time.

It was a nice, steady journey with no turbulence. When the plane had landed, Uncle Gino met her in the reception. He was very pleased to see her on the way to the vineyard where she was going to stay: the house where her mother and father occupied when they were alive. At that time, she was really excited and looking forward to meeting all of her relatives. Uncle Gino carried in her bags and showed her to her old room for the two weeks of her stay.

Uncle Gino said to Maria, 'I hope you have a good stay'.

Maria answered, 'Thank you Uncle'.

Gino took her bags to her old room. 'I hope you have a nice stay. I will see you in the morning at breakfast'.

She was very excited and she looked out the window and could see how nice it all looked. It was a very sunny day and, in the background, one of the fields contained grapevines. The sun was shining on the grapes and they all looked stunning.

Maria went down to the kitchen and made herself some coffee. She also got something to eat, then she met the wife of the owner of the vineyard. It was the first time that she had met them personally. Mr Alessia and Mrs Alessia were the new owners of the vineyard; Mrs Alessia said, 'Welcome, Maria. Nice to meet you'.

Maria replied, 'It is nice to meet you. Thank you for letting me stay with you'.

Mrs Alessia greeted Maria, cuddled her, and in broken Italian—she could not speak much English, just a little—said, 'It is nice to have you come to stay with us. Please make yourself welcome and help yourself to hot drinks and biscuits, which are all in the cupboard'.

Mr Alessia shook Maria by the hand and also kissed her on the side of the cheek.

'I hope you enjoy the countryside and that you make yourself at home here'.

'Thank you', Maria answered. 'I am really looking forward to having a nice holiday with you and your wife'.

Mrs Alessia replied, 'I am deeply sorry about your parents who passed'.

Maria said, 'That's kind of you. I miss my parents very much'.

Mrs Alessia said, 'If there is anything I can do please let me know'.

Maria spent most of the day walking around the garden and having a look at some of the grapevines that were shining in the sun. How wonderful, she thought. It was nice to be back home. She kept thinking about her patients at the care home, and she was wondering how Jimmy was getting on. Also, how Mrs. Wentworth was. She was hoping that they were being well looked after and that they would still be there when she arrived home. She could not get them out of her mind because she was so attached to her favourite patients.

Before she went to bed, she unpacked her suitcase and folded and hung her belongings in the wardrobe.

Evening time came, and she decided she would go to bed early. After the trip, she felt really tired, and on Sunday she would be able to go to the local church that she used to attend when she lived in that area. She was wondering who the priest would be. Maria was quite lucky because she could speak perfect Italian, so she would be able to understand the Mass, and then she could talk to other churchgoers.

The morning soon came around. Maria woke up early because she wanted to go to the early church service for the Mass, although, she did not speak to the priest because he was too busy. Some of the congregation recognised Maria; when the Mass was finished they came up to her, and gathered around her. Some of them knew her mother and father because they used to attend the same church. They made quite a fuss around her. Maria shook everyone's hand and told them it was nice to see them all.

After the church service, Maria was going with Mr. Alessia to visit some of the vineyards, and then on Sunday morning, she was going to attend the meeting with the other shareholders of the vineyards. She went down to the dining area—breakfast was already waiting for her. Uncle Genio was already having his breakfast, like he always did before he went to work in the vineyard. After breakfast, Maria decided she would go and visit all her relatives who lived in the area. She met so many uncles and aunts—they all made her feel very welcome. She stayed, had drinks with them, then had to get back to the house for the meeting.

She got back to the house; some of the other shareholders were already there, drinking coffee and chatting, and they were all sitting around the table waiting for her to join the meeting. Everything was explained: they were going to buy some other vineyards in the nearby areas of the villages. The shareholders were told they would need more vineyards if they were going to export to other countries like Great Britain. Maria didn't say very much; she just listened to what the proposals were. She agreed it was a good idea that this should happen, and when they asked her for her opinion, she said she was happy to go along with their proposals.

After the meeting, a coach took all the shareholders on a tour of the other vineyards they planned to buy.

Maria stayed silent, astonished by their plan to buy so many vineyards, completing the plan. Shareholders will help new owners with the paperwork.

Maria was told that she would receive a yearly balance of any profits that were made from exporting the wine; she would get a share. Maria was delighted with that, as she said it would help her in the future in England. The two weeks seemed to fly by, and she had one of the most enjoyable holidays; she thanked the new owners, she told them that she had a wonderful holiday and that she was hoping she could see them again soon. They all shook hands, and Uncle Gino took her to the airport.

It was now time for her to catch the plane and returned to England she said goodbye to Uncle Gino he said take care of yourself Maria, I will see you soon she turned to him and smiled and said to him, I have had a wonderful holiday please take care of yourself and look after the vineyard for me.

Chapter 6
Returning Home

Maria was returning home, and while she was sitting on the plane, she began to think about many things. The one person most on her mind was the leading actor, Timothy Daly. She was wondering what had happened in the episodes of her favourite television programme, *Down in the Country*.

She had missed quite a few episodes and couldn't wait to return home so she could catch up on what was happening. She thought to herself, *I've missed watching Dr Timothy and how things are going with the affair he's having with one of his patients.* Although she didn't think it was right for him to have such an affair—he could be struck off—Maria wouldn't have liked that. She was so in love with Dr Timothy. She had been watching that programme for a very long time.

If only I could meet him, she said to herself.

One day, she planned to go and see the programme recorded live at the television studio. She knew they often invited audiences to attend. In the meantime, she thought she would write him a letter asking for a signed photo. As soon as she got back home, she would do just that.

The plane landed, and she caught a taxi to her flat. She was relieved the journey was over and could now settle down, thinking about writing the letter to her favourite actor.

She also began thinking about her favourite patients. While shopping in Italy, she had bought three presents for them.

It had been difficult for Maria to choose suitable gifts due to her clients' conditions, but she managed to find three thoughtful presents, and she couldn't wait to give them out. She was also excited to tell her friend, Pauline Watson, about her trip to Italy.

Once Maria had settled in at her flat and unpacked her case, the first thing she did was sit down and write a letter to the studio where her favourite programme was being recorded.

Dear Timothy,

'I really enjoy the programme that you take part in'.

'I try never to miss an episode because I love your performances'.

'You are one of my favourite actors, and the part you play is tremendous'.

'I was wondering if you would be kind enough to send me a signed photo'.

Yours faithfully,
Maria Giovanni.

Without delay, she went to the local post box and posted the letter. As she walked home, she wondered if she would receive a reply—she certainly hoped so.

She decided to visit the Care Home and check in on the patients she had been looking after before officially starting work again on Monday morning. When she arrived, she was relieved to see that her three favourite patients were keeping very well. She visited each of them and gave them their gifts, which they could place on their bedside tables as a reminder of Maria. Pauline wasn't on duty, so Maria didn't stay long. She decided she would wait until Monday to catch up with her properly.

Since the day was warm, she decided to go and sit on the beach for a couple of hours. She took her chair and settled in her favourite spot, looking out at the sea while reading a magazine. Suddenly, a man approached her.

'Would you mind if I sit near you?' he asked.

'No, that's perfectly OK', Maria answered.

After a little while, he turned to Maria and said, 'This is a wonderful place, this beach'.

'Yes', said Maria. 'I come here a lot'.

'My name is Jack', he said to her, 'and I'm pleased to meet you'.

Maria turned her head a bit hesitantly.

'My name is Maria', she answered.

He reached over and shook her hand.

I really like this beach. It's nice and quiet, and it doesn't get very crowded'.

Maria nodded.

'No, that's one of the reasons I like coming here', she replied.

He added, 'The beaches are lovely and clean. The council keeps them in good condition, and it's really nice to see'.

Maria didn't like talking much when she came to the beach—she just liked to rest. Still, Jack continued speaking, and she listened, even though she didn't want to answer many of his questions. She felt obliged to respond. In the end, she was glad he had spoken to her and that she had managed to join in the conversation. She wasn't used to talking to people she didn't know.

'I come from London originally', Jack told her. 'I live here now, in Ramsgate'.

'That's nice', she commented.

After a little while, she said, 'I'll see you again. I have to go now'.

'OK', he replied. 'I'll see you here again sometime'.

'More than likely', Maria said.

Chapter 7
Friendship

Maria started work on Monday morning. She was feeling relaxed and rested. She knew it was going to be a hard day because she had to do the rounds and see as many patients as she could. She arrived early, and waiting for her was her friend Pauline.

'Good morning, Pauline', Maria said.
'Good morning, Maria. Did you have a good holiday?'

Maria replied with a smile, 'Yes, it was marvellous. I saw lots of my relatives and the new owners of the vineyard. We had a very good meeting. The weather was brilliant, and the sun was shining every day'.

'That's good', said Pauline. 'It's been very busy here, and we've missed you'.

Maria was delighted to see Pauline again after her two-week holiday.

'Maria, I have some important news to tell you. Mrs Watson is not very well. She took a turn for the worse last night, and we've made her comfortable. I think she's only going to be with us for a day or so'.

Maria was upset by the news. She went straight into Catherine's room to see her. She held her hand and quietly said a small prayer. She could see that Catherine was slipping away.

Maria felt her pulse and could tell it was very slow. She made sure she was comfortable, straightened her bed, and adjusted her pillow. Then she left the room, feeling very sad. Maria had liked Catherine, but she thought to herself, *At least now she will have peace.*

Maria called the doctor who was on duty, and he came to see Catherine. He told Maria that he had given her some medication to ease any pain she might have. Maria was pleased that she would be comfortable.

She and Pauline carried out their routine rounds, checking on the clients and making sure they all had the right amount of medication.

After Maria's shift ended, she decided to sit on the beach for a couple of hours. She went to her favourite spot. After a little while, to Maria's surprise, Jack appeared and sat beside her.

'Hello, Maria', he said. 'Sorry, I'm a bit late. I got delayed at work'.

Maria answered, 'That's OK. I was wondering if you were coming. It's such a beautiful day today'.

Jack sat down in his chair, right next to Maria. She was a bit surprised by how close he was.

'What have you been doing today?' asked Maria.

'One of the gym users hurt his back while lifting heavy weights. He came to see me, and it was a little late. I gave him some advice, and he's coming back in a few days. That's when I'll give him a sports massage to help him get better quicker'.

'That would be nice', Maria said.

They had many conversations. Maria felt they were becoming good friends.

'Maria, can you meet me next week? I'll bring a picnic, and we can have something nice to eat and drink'.

'OK, Jack, that will be fine. I'll just check what shift I'm on'. After looking at her diary, she said, 'That's fine. On Tuesday, I finish at 3:00 p.m.—can we meet then?'

Jack replied, 'Yes'.

'OK', Maria said. 'That'll give us a couple of hours to have something to eat and drink'.

'I must go now', said Maria. 'It's time for my favourite television programme'.

With that, they both packed away their chairs and said goodbye. Jack reached over and gave Maria a small kiss on the cheek. She felt very pleased that someone was making a fuss of her. On her way back to the flat, she couldn't stop thinking about Jack and the fact that she was going to meet him again next week.

She started to feel confused. *What am I doing?* she said to herself.

Back at the flat, Maria got ready to watch her programme, *Down in the Country*. She had an evening meal and then settled down. She turned on the television and waited for the show to start. The episode opened with Dr Timothy Daly's surgery.

Halfway through the programme, Maria felt a great attraction to Timothy. She wondered what it would be like to make love to him. She closed her eyes and imagined being held in his arms. The feeling of excitement overwhelmed her, and she couldn't help feeling aroused. A deep sensation came over her. Without hesitation, her hand moved slowly between her thighs, pressing gently. She was lost in thoughts of him, and the sensations intensified. Her hand moved faster and faster until she reached a powerful release, followed by a sense of relief.

After the programme, Maria felt even more in love with the doctor. She decided she must see him live in the studio. She had heard that the television company occasionally invited people to be part of the audience during a recording, and she would make inquiries to find out how to go about it.

The next day, Maria began her shift at the Care Home. One of the care assistants greeted her and informed her of the sad news that Catherine had passed away at 4:00 a.m.

Maria wasn't surprised; she had expected it.

The care assistant added, 'Her husband is on his way to say his final goodbyes'.

Maria went into the bedroom to see Catherine. She looked very peaceful. Maria held her hand and said, 'Goodbye, my friend', and made the sign of the cross. Then she left the room.

She went into the staff restroom, where Pauline Watson was waiting to talk.

'Catherine passed away this morning', Maria said.

'She was a lovely woman', Pauline replied. 'I believe the undertakers are coming at 11:00 a.m., after her husband has left'.

Maria and Pauline continued with their rounds at the Care Home. Maria had another favourite lady she looked after—Ann Davis, who suffered from diabetes.

Maria made sure she had all her medication and helped her check her blood sugar levels. Ann was in her late 80s, held her age very well, and was well cared for. She had a lovely family who visited her regularly. But due to her arthritis, she had great difficulty walking and couldn't cope alone. Together with her family's support and consent, she decided that moving into Southfields Care Home was the best decision.

Chapter 8
Good News

The manager came to see Maria and told her there was going to be a change at the Care Home. The National Health Service had approached them and wanted to take over part of the Care Home. They wished to convert some of the facility for mental health patients who suffer from various conditions, not acute, but ongoing.

Maria listened intently to what Ben was telling her. He explained that the shareholders were very pleased this was going to happen, as they had applied to the National Health Service to express interest.

Ben said, 'The shareholders have asked me to speak to you and see if you would like to be upgraded and take over the management of that side of the Care Home. Most of the patients coming from the NHS will have mental health issues like depression, bipolar disorder, and other conditions. We are prepared to send you on specialist training courses in this area. You will be on a higher grade, so you will be well compensated. What do you think?'

Maria answered, 'I think that would be a wonderful opportunity for me to advance in my career. I had been thinking about exploring new positions, and this could be the perfect step forward. I've always been interested in helping people with mental health problems. I know a few people who suffer from mental illness, and they've told me about the tribulations they face'.

'I'm happy to accept the position. Can you tell me when this will start? Will my conditions of service remain the same, even though this is a different role? I would really like to keep everything as is'.

Ben replied, 'Your conditions of service will be exactly the same because you'll still be working for the same company, so there's no need to worry about that'.

'I haven't got a specific start date yet', he added, 'but I know some building work will begin soon, and this will give you time to attend training courses in mental health care'.

Maria was excited about the prospect, and she thanked Ben for the opportunity.

She went straight away to tell Pauline the good news. Pauline was very pleased for her, though she expressed concern that she might not see Maria as much.

'Don't worry', Maria said. 'I'll make sure we're not separated, especially since it's just a different part of the Care Home'.

Pauline was very happy to hear that.

Back at the flat, Maria was getting ready for another day at the Care Home when the postman delivered her letters. On opening them, she found a large envelope that caught her attention. She opened it and found a photograph inside—it was a signed photo from Timothy Daly, her favourite actor. She was delighted. Inside the envelope was also a small letter:

Dear Maria,

Thank you for your letter. I'm glad that you are enjoying the programme, and I'm happy to send this photo to you, which I have signed personally.

I hope you continue to enjoy the TV programme. Please find enclosed two tickets to be part of the audience when the

programme is being recorded. I'll be happy to meet you and say hello when the show finishes.

Yours faithfully,
Eddie Price.

Maria could not believe she had received two tickets to see Eddie in the TV series. She looked at the date—it was in three weeks' time.

I can't believe this is happening to me, she said to herself. *What shall I wear?*

She wandered around, daydreaming—finally, she was going to meet her favourite actor.

Suddenly, Maria realised it was Wednesday, and she had to go to the beach to meet Jack. After finishing her shift for the day, she drove to the beach and set up her chair. There was no sign of Jack. She felt a little disappointed but began to relax. Then, suddenly, he appeared.

'Hello, Maria', he said. 'Sorry, I'm a bit late—I got delayed by work'.

Maria answered, 'That's OK. I was wondering if you were coming. It's such a beautiful day today'.

He sat down on his chair, right next to Maria. She was a bit surprised by how close he was to her.

'What have you been doing today?' asked Maria.

'One of the gym users hurt his back while lifting heavy weights. He came to see me, and it was a bit late. I gave him some advice, and he's coming back in a few days. That's when I'll give him a sports massage to help him recover quicker'.

'That would be nice', Maria said.

They had many conversations, and Maria felt they were becoming good friends.

'Maria, can you meet me next week? I'll bring a picnic, and we can have something nice to eat and drink'.

'OK, Jack, that will be fine. I'll just check to see what shift I'm on'. After looking at her diary, she said, 'That's fine. On Tuesday, I finish at 3:00 p.m. Can we meet then?'

Jack replied, 'Yes'.

'OK', Maria said. 'That'll give us a couple of hours to have something to eat and drink'.

'I must go now', said Maria. 'It's time to watch my favourite television programme'.

With that, they both packed away their chairs and said goodbye. Jack reached over and gave Maria a small kiss on the cheek. She felt very pleased that someone was making a fuss over her.

On her way back to the flat, she could not stop thinking about Jack and that she was going to meet him again next week. She started to feel confused.

What am I doing? she said to herself.

Chapter 9
New Arrivals

The day started with Catherine's funeral. They always tried to attend funerals when people from the Care Home passed away. This was no exception. Maria was quite fond of Catherine Watson. There weren't many people at the funeral—just a few of her relatives. The manager of the Care Home, Ben, went with Maria. It was a very solemn occasion. The local priest conducted the service and said Catherine was a wonderful person who had worked all her life. She didn't ask for much; she simply went about bringing up her family and doing the best she could. After the service had finished at the local church, she was laid to rest in a private ceremony.

Maria and Ben went to a local café and had coffee. They talked about Catherine. Maria told Ben that she would miss her—she was always smiling despite her illnesses.

It was time for Maria to start work. She had been told beforehand that a very unusual circumstance was about to happen at the Care Home. Two more clients were coming: Mr and Mrs Rogers. Mr Eric Rogers was going to be brought by ambulance, having just been discharged from the local General Hospital. He had an accident at home and had been admitted to the hospital, complaining of back pain and an inability to walk.

Mr Rogers was a very stubborn man. He refused to let the hospital treat him or investigate the problem. The hospital wanted to do a scan, but he wouldn't allow it. He was quite an eccentric person—86 years old—and would not even let the hospital do anything for him whatsoever. He was in the hospital for rehabilitation, but because no treatment could be done, they sent him to Southfields Care Home to be looked after. By this time, he was completely bedridden and had to be assisted with everything.

The next day, his wife, Cheryl Rogers, was admitted to the Care Home as well. She had been living on her own and could no longer cope with daily tasks. She was a very nervous person and relied heavily on antidepressants and other drugs prescribed by her doctors. As a result, she had become addicted to her medication. She would not even dress herself and would stay in her nightgown and dressing gown. Their daughter and son-in-law lived far away in Surrey and could not visit them often.

The doctor and Maria went to see Eric to give him an examination and try to determine what was wrong. Maria talked with him for a little while and discovered how stubborn he was. He would hardly tell the doctor anything about his life. When Maria asked about his past medical history, he refused to answer. They decided to leave him for now and let him settle into life at the Care Home. The doctor listened to his chest to check for any infection, but the result was negative.

Then the doctor and Maria went to see Cheryl. They found her to be extremely nervous and unable to communicate properly. They were unable to explain why she was at the Care Home. Cheryl had to be looked after. She inquired about her husband.

'He's fine and settled in well', replied Maria.

'Cheryl, can you tell me why you won't get dressed?'

Cheryl replied, 'I can't be bothered. I really don't want to be here. When can I go home?'

The doctor left the room, and Maria stayed behind, talking to Cheryl.

'You'll like it here. There are lots of people you can become friendly with, and you'll be well looked after'.

Cheryl answered, 'I don't care. Will I be getting my drugs?'

'Yes, we'll look after your medication and make sure you get what you need', Maria assured her.

Mr and Mrs Rogers had a lovely bungalow where they had lived for forty years. The only problem was that the bungalow had to be sold to help pay for their care. Mrs Rogers understood, but she was still very upset. She knew she would never return to the bungalow.

Eric used to do a lot of gardening and took pride in maintaining the bungalow. He was quite proud of his garden. He was a very clever man and used to paint portraits of Native Americans, which fascinated him. Some of his artwork was outstanding. He also did a lot of embroidery with different threads and was very talented with his sewing, mostly on jackets, often depicting Native American themes. When he went shopping, people would often ask him if he had done the sewing on his clothes.

A few years ago, he had a stroke, which prevented him from painting and sewing. He became quite handicapped. He wasn't overly concerned about the bungalow and had left all the arrangements to his wife.

Cheryl and Eric had a very good friend, their neighbour Kerry Williamson, who used to look after them when they lived in the bungalow. Kerry often took them out for lunch and was quite upset when they were moved to Southfields Care Home. A few days after their admission, Kerry visited them both to see how they were getting on. She brought them treats so they could enjoy something nice to eat. Kerry thought it was a pity that their daughter and son-in-law couldn't visit. She felt it was very sad that her two friends were now alone in the Care Home with no family visiting.

Eric's condition took a turn for the worse. He wasn't eating and was losing a lot of weight. His children were notified about his condition, but they responded that they were both working and couldn't get time off. They asked the Care Home to keep them informed of any further changes.

Maria knew that Mrs Kerry Williamson would visit regularly, so she informed her of Eric's condition. Unfortunately, Eric's health declined further, and he passed away in his sleep. It was very sad for the nurses and care staff to witness someone suffer in that way. His family was notified and made the necessary arrangements for his remains.

Mrs Rogers was very upset that her husband had passed on. Kerry, her neighbour, continued to visit and tried to comfort her as much as she could. Sadly, the visits were beginning to affect Kerry emotionally. Each time she saw Mrs Rogers, she would go home quite depressed. It was hard for her to see her old friend suffer so much, especially knowing how much she hated being in the Care Home.

Still, Kerry carried on visiting Mrs Rogers, and she always looked forward to her visits. If Kerry didn't come, Mrs Rogers would ask the Care Home to telephone her to ask when she would next visit. Kerry would usually reply that she would try to come every Wednesday.

Chapter 10
Maria's First Real Date

Maria finished her shift at the Care Home. She was excited that she was meeting Jack later on. She told Pauline that she was going on a date with Jack. Pauline was excited for her and wished her the best of luck.

Maria made herself look as nice as she could. She then went to the beach. After sitting down on the beach, Jack appeared carrying a picnic basket.

'Hello Maria, how are you today?' said Jack.

Maria replied promptly. 'I'm fine. What have you got in that basket, Jack?' she said.

'I thought I'd bring a picnic. I hope you're hungry', Jack replied.

Maria smiled. She didn't say much because she was extremely nervous. She was thinking to herself, *Am I doing the right thing by encouraging Jack to meet me?*

Jack put the basket down and opened it. He took out a tablecloth and laid it on the sand. Maria looked at all the good things to eat. He had cooked chicken, pork pies, biscuits, cheese, and tomatoes.

'Get stuck in', Jack said, as he poured out coffee. 'I hope you like coffee', Jack said.

'Yes, I love coffee', answered Maria.

They were both enjoying the food Jack had prepared. Maria started to feel relaxed, and she was happy that Jack was with her. The conversation continued for the next hour. After they had finished the food, Jack moved his chair very close to Maria.

'Do you remember that man who hurt his back lifting heavy weights I told you about? I managed to make him feel so much better today, and he was ever so grateful. I gave him a massage, and afterwards he told me that he had no pain'.

'That was good', said Maria. 'I bet he was pleased'.

Jack replied, 'Yes, he was. Maria, have you ever had a massage?'

'No, it's not something I've got into, but I suppose it would be pretty nice'.

'I took a course in massage therapy a few years ago. Would you like me to give you a massage sometime?' Jack offered.

'I'd have to think about that', she said with a little giggle.

After two hours, they decided they'd had a nice day.

'Don't forget, Maria, what I said—I'd love to give you a massage sometime. Just let me know'.

Maria replied, 'OK, Jack. I might take you up on that'.

Maria was quite busy with work, and she hadn't had time to make another date with Jack, but it kept coming into her mind—if she would see him again on the beach. She was certainly hoping so.

She told Pauline all about the date with Jack. Pauline was quite envious. Pauline hadn't got a boyfriend, but she wished she had, and she told Maria how lucky she was to have somebody paying her attention.

'I think you should see if you can find him on the beach again. He seemed like a nice person', Pauline told Maria.

'Yes', she said. 'I must see if I can see him. I might even take him up on his offer', she added with a chuckle.

Chapter 11
Jimmy

Maria was very busy that day at work at the Care Home. She took the opportunity to go into Jimmy's room. He was suffering from COPD. Maria always liked to talk to him because he was such an interesting person, and he enjoyed her visits regularly.

Maria knocked at his door to make sure he was OK.

'Hello, Jimmy', Maria said. 'How are you today, lovely?'

He replied, 'I'm not feeling too good, to be honest, Maria. I'm having a lot of problems with my breathing, and it's extremely hard for me to get my breath'.

'Have you been taking your inhalers?' Maria asked.

'Yes, I have, but they don't seem to be having the same effect as they used to'.

'Never mind', commented Maria. 'I'll fix you up with a nebuliser. I'll be back in ten minutes, so if you hold on, I'll get it for you'.

'Please, Maria, will you wait a while? I have something important to tell you'.

She wondered what Jimmy wanted—what could be so important to him? She pulled up a chair next to his bed.

'I really should be getting you this nebuliser. It will make you feel much better'.

'No matter', Jimmy said. 'You know that I am very fond of you, Maria'.

'Are you?' said Maria.

'I am. I'm at that age where I have to be realistic about my condition. It's getting worse, and every day I struggle, especially with my breathing. I want to tell you something, in case anything happens to me'.

'What is that, Jimmy?' Maria inquired.

'I want to look after you. I want to make sure that you will have plenty of money when you finish nursing. I've decided I will leave you all that I have. I have made a will, and you will be the beneficiary. I have no relations—my wife has passed on—so I am making this will so you will inherit all my estate'.

She didn't know what to say. She was dumbfounded at this suggestion from Jimmy.

'You don't have to do that', she said. 'Are you sure no relatives would receive help from your estate?'

'I am certain, and this is what I want. Please go to the cupboard and open the drawer. You will find a tin. Open the lid—you'll find six medals which I received when I was in World War II'.

Maria took out the tin and gave it to Jimmy. He took out the medals and held them in front of Maria.

'Some of these have no value', he said. 'Some have a little value, but this one is very special'.

He held it out.

'Do you know what this is, Maria?'

'No, Jimmy', she said. 'I don't know anything about medals'.

'Well, Maria, this is the Victoria Cross. I was awarded it for bravery. I never wanted this medal, but the army was proud to present it to me'.

'What did you do to get this medal?' Maria asked.

'We were under heavy fire. Three of my comrades were badly wounded. I did what any other soldier would have done—I just went over to them and carried them back, one by one, to safety, doing the best I could. I must have saved their lives, because they were taken to hospital, and I understand that they survived. A piece of shrapnel hit me on the shoulder, and I still managed to carry the soldiers to safety'.

'I know this medal is worth a great deal of money, and you can sell it and invest the money for your future. If you look back into the drawer, you can see the will, which is addressed to "Whom It May Concern"'.

'Jimmy, I don't know what to say', commented Maria. 'That is exceedingly kind of you. Are you sure, Jimmy, that you want to do that?'

'Don't say anything', said Jimmy. 'I must tell you. I look upon you as if you are my daughter. I hope you don't mind that'.

Maria commented, 'I feel very privileged that you've said that, Jimmy. It's my job to look after you and to make sure that you are well'.

'Just promise me, Maria, when my time comes, please hand this letter to the administrators of my estate. Will you promise me that?'

'Yes, I will. And don't worry', answered Maria. 'Now I must get your nebuliser. I'll be back in ten minutes with it'.

Maria left the room. She was still thinking about what he had told her.

Maria returned and sat beside Jimmy. She fixed up his nebuliser and turned it on. Jimmy felt much better—he could breathe much more easily. She sat with him for twenty minutes and helped him take off the nebuliser from his mouth. He was breathing much better.

She held his hand and said to him, 'You'll be OK. I'll see you later. I have to go and see some more patients'.

Chapter 12
The Studio

The day had come for Maria to go to the studio to be in the audience for the performance of *Down in the Country*. She had tickets and was very excited at the prospect of meeting her heart's desire, Eddie Price. She had told Pauline that she was going to see the programme and that she had two tickets. She asked Pauline if she wanted to come with her.

'I'm on duty', Pauline answered. 'I am so sorry. I would have loved to come with you, Maria'.

She decided that she would have to go on her own. She set off to the studio and arrived at 11:00 a.m. She was greeted by the commissioner, who showed her where to sit. She knew she would be there most of the day, as one episode would be recorded in a day.

Other people arrived and took their seats, and they all settled down, waiting for the programme to start. The producer spoke to all the guests and told them that during the performance, they would have to keep quiet and not clap at all.

The performance started, and suddenly Eddie appeared to take his part. Maria's heart sank as she watched him. During the performance, she thought to herself that he was much more handsome in real life than on television, and she was hoping that she could get to talk to him after it was all over. The producer had told them they could mix with the stars after the show was recorded.

Eventually, after several hours, the producer said the audience was invited to meet in the studio bar with the actors and actresses.

Some people were sitting down at the tables in the bar, and some were standing. Maria was standing by the bar. Eddie was talking to quite a few of the guests. He came over to Maria.

'Hello, how are you today, and did you enjoy the performance?' commented Eddie.

Maria answered a little bit nervously and said, 'Yes, it was nice. I loved your part in the programme'.

'That is nice', he said. 'What is your name?'

Maria answered, 'I did send you a letter asking for your photo, which you kindly sent to me, and the tickets. I would like to thank you for that'.

'You are very welcome', replied Eddie. 'I noticed in your letter you said you watched the programme quite often'.

'Yes', she answered. 'I never miss an episode'.

'I am very honoured', replied Eddie. 'Would you like a drink, Maria?'

'That is kind of you. May I call you "Eddie"?'

'Yes, certainly'.

'I would love a shandy', said Maria, and with that, Eddie ordered a shandy and a drink for himself.

'Shall we sit down?' asked Eddie.

'Yes, that would be nice'.

They found a table, sat down, and started a conversation. He must have been with Maria for at least half an hour. Maria was so excited. After many years of watching the programme, she was now talking to Eddie. She was so surprised when he turned round to her and said he would like her phone number and would phone her sometime to see how she was getting on.

She told him she was a nurse at the Care Home. He was very interested in what she was telling him about the Care Home.

'My mother is in a Care Home in London, so I know all about how Care Homes work. I visit her quite regularly', he said.

They exchanged phone numbers, and with that Eddie said, 'I must go now. I have to do an interview later for the radio'.

Maria made her way back to her flat. She could not believe what had happened and that she had his phone number. She could not wait to go to work to tell Pauline all about it.

Chapter 13
Hospital

Jimmy West from the Care Home took a turn for the worse, and he was suffering with his breathing. The Care Home called an ambulance, and the paramedics took him straight to hospital after they conducted routine checks on him.

After being in hospital for a few days, he started to improve. They were treating him with antibiotics and steroids. Jimmy was lying in his bed, but he started to get very restless, tossing and turning, and he was sweating quite a lot. He got out of bed and started to walk up and down the ward very slowly. He began to have hallucinations and thought he was in prison.

One of the nurses came up to him and said, 'What is the matter, Jimmy? You look a bit confused, love'.

Jimmy turned round to her and said, 'I know what you have done. You have killed one of the patients'.

'What do you mean, Jimmy?'

Jimmy replied, 'I have seen you with the patient, and he has died. You have killed him. I will report you to the police'.

'Do not be silly. Get back to bed', the nurse said.

She told the sister what was happening to Jimmy, that he was acting very strangely. The nurses did not realise what was happening to him—he was having a psychotic episode due to his medication. Taking steroids can cause this in certain people.

It had never happened at this hospital before.

Jimmy was completely out of it. He phoned the police several times, complaining that someone had stolen his car. The police phoned the hospital to find out what the situation was. The sister explained that it was a patient who was going through a mental block and not to take any notice of his phone calls.

The police said, 'Can't you take away his phone?'

The sister answered, 'No, we are not allowed. The only thing we can hope for is that his phone goes dead and he cannot make any calls'.

Jimmy went to the nurses' station, hardly able to walk. He told them he wanted to go home. The nurse on duty said that he would have to fill in a special form and see the doctor before they could do that.

The doctor was called, and he said Jimmy was in no state to go home. With that, Jimmy left the nurses' station. He tried to walk out of the ward and attempted to open the double doors. The doors had a special lock that required a code to open. He couldn't open the door, so he walked into the shower room. He nearly fell over but managed to save himself from injury. Jimmy was exhausted and managed to sit down on a small seat.

The nurses tried to persuade him to come out, but they couldn't succeed, so they had to call the security team. Jimmy's psychotic episode was getting worse. Eventually, they got him back into bed, and they had to call the duty psychiatrist. She asked Jimmy a few questions and prescribed him medication.

They had to hold him down with several nurses and two security guards to give him an injection to make him sleep. While this was happening, Jimmy struggled to get free and suddenly kicked the tray from the doctor's hands. It flew into the air and landed on the bed. The doctor managed to retrieve the injection and gave it to him in his bottom.

They all left, and Jimmy was lying there on his own with his phone. He was rubbing his backside, trying to stop the injection from working, and he thought he would get his own back by playing his favourite singer, Bob Marley, on his phone as loud as he could. Unfortunately, one of the nurses commented that Bob Marley was one of her favourite singers.

After a little while, Jimmy fell asleep. When he came around the next morning, the bed was in turmoil. He felt much better and like his old self.

The nurse said to him, 'You'd better apologise to Nurse Williams for what you said to her'.

Later in the day, when she came on duty, he called over to her.

'Nurse Williams', he said, 'I must apologise to you for what I said to you'.

He was quite upset after the nurses had told him what he had said to Nurse Williams. She totally understood.

She said, 'Do not worry. I've forgotten all about it. It's part of the job'.

Days later, Jimmy was discharged and returned to the Care Home. Maria went to see Jimmy and said, 'I heard you had a funny episode'.

'Yes', said Jimmy. 'I can't remember much about it, but I know I made a nuisance of myself'.

'Don't worry about that, Jimmy. The nurses understand. They're used to that type of thing'.

She made sure he was comfortable and then went to see her other clients.

Chapter 14
Phone Call

Maria was getting ready to go to work the next day when the phone started to ring.

'Hello, Maria speaking'.

'Hi, this is Eddie. How are you? It's Eddie from the TV show'.

'Hello! How are you getting on?' answered Maria.

'I'm fine', he said. 'I've been thinking about you and thought I must give you a ring. It was nice talking to you after the show. I'm doing a television commercial in Margate and was wondering if you'd like to come and have coffee with me. It's only a half-hour drive from Margate to where you are. What do you think?'

'Yes, that's a lovely idea. I'm so pleased you phoned. I've been thinking about you too'.

'Have you?' he said. 'That's good. Where would you like me to come and meet you?'

She replied, 'There's a nice little coffee shop in the High Street. It's called Joe's Coffee House'.

Eddie said, 'The commercial is being recorded next week, so I can come next Wednesday, if that suits you'.

'That's fine', she replied. 'Would 2:00 p.m. be okay? I should be finished with work by 1:00 p.m.'

'OK, I'll see you then', he replied.

With that, the phone call ended. She was delighted and couldn't wait to go to work and tell Pauline.

'Guess what? I have a date with Eddie next Wednesday!'

'You lucky thing', Pauline answered. 'I hope it all goes well for you'.

Wednesday morning came around. Maria was on her usual shift, due to finish at 1:00 p.m., but she was so excited she could hardly concentrate. She was jittery, and when her shift ended, she went into the restroom to check her appearance before meeting Eddie.

She said to herself, *What should I say to him?*

She made her way to the coffee shop, and when she arrived, Eddie was already there, drinking coffee. When he saw her, he stood up and kissed her on the cheek.

'Thank you, darling, for coming', he said. 'What would you like to drink?'

'I'll have a latte, please'.

He ordered her latte and they sat down together, chatting about all sorts of things, including the new commercial he was filming. They got on very well, and after about an hour, Eddie said, 'I must go now. Maria, can I see you again? I'd like to take you out to dinner'.

'Yes, that would be lovely', she answered.

They arranged a time and date. Eddie kissed her on the cheek again and said, 'Maria, I'll see you in two weeks' time. In the meantime, I'll phone you and book a table'.

They walked out together and waved goodbye. Maria was so excited. As she walked home to her flat, all she could think about was Eddie.

The next day, she returned to work and went to check on Jimmy. He was asleep, so she didn't disturb him, but she could see he didn't look very well. He hadn't been eating much, and Maria was quite concerned. She discussed Jimmy's condition with the manager, Ben.

Ben said, 'Jimmy looks like he's slipping away'.

'Oh dear', replied Maria.

She understood, of course. Jimmy was at an age where this sort of thing could happen. She told Pauline and asked her to keep an eye on him and make sure he was comfortable.

A few days later, Jimmy passed away peacefully in his sleep.

Maria was with him when it happened. It was the first time in her nursing career that she had felt truly upset when a patient passed away. To her, Jimmy wasn't just a patient. He had become a great friend.

The undertakers came the next day to collect Jimmy and take him to the Chapel of Rest. Ben, the care home manager, arranged the funeral as instructed by Jimmy's solicitor.

After Jimmy left, the Care Home staff gathered his belongings and stored them in the office. Jimmy had made arrangements for a solicitor to handle his affairs. He still owned a house in Ramsgate, which the solicitors at Jeffries were now responsible for. After the undertakers had removed Jimmy's body, the staff cleaned his room and prepared it for the next patient.

Maria and Pauline were sitting in the staff room, having coffee.

'It's so sad when someone passes and they have no relatives to take care of their possessions', Maria commented.

'Will you be going to the funeral?' asked Pauline.

'Yes, I will. I don't suppose there will be many people there. As soon as I hear the date, I'll let you know. Would you like to come with me?'

'Yes, I would', Pauline answered.

Not long after, the care home was notified of the date for Jimmy's funeral.

Maria, Pauline, the manager, and one of the care assistants attended the service at the crematorium. Maria was quite surprised when they brought the coffin into the chapel. A group of soldiers lined the entrance, and his coffin was draped with the Union Jack. She was deeply moved to see that he was being given a military send-off.

The Army chaplain from Jimmy's old regiment conducted the service. He spoke about Jimmy's bravery, and his medals were placed on top of the coffin. A photo of Jimmy in his army uniform, taken when he was a young man, was displayed beside it.

After Jimmy was laid to rest, everyone said their goodbyes. Ben Hutchinson thanked those who had come and expressed special appreciation to the Army chaplain for the beautiful service.

Chapter 15
Builders

Maria was on her last day of training regarding mental health issues, and she understood the ramifications of what is needed when somebody has to come into a care home with mental issues. She was very pleased that she had been given the job of the Head Nurse and was running the department. She knew that it was going to be a challenge and that she would have to employ some more staff with experience in looking after people with mental issues. The local hospital would refer patients to the care home after they had been discharged from hospital and needed further help. It was going to be a completely new role for her.

The building contractors were already working on the new section of the care home, and it would be completed in about three weeks. She went to have a look to see how they were progressing. She was very pleased with the work that they had done. She was shown her office that she would be using; all the equipment was being put in place, which was sanctioned by the NHS.

All the building work that was taking place was overseen by the clerk of works from the National Health Service. Maria had finished her shift. She decided that she would go and sit on the beach for a couple of hours before she went home. It was a nice sunny day, and she just wanted to relax and enjoy herself sitting in the sun.

After an hour, Jack was approaching her. He came and sat next to her.

'Hello Maria'.

'Have not seen you for a long time', said Jack.

'Oh', she said. 'I have been terribly busy. Lots of things have happened. How are you, Jack?' she commented.

'I am fine. I have been busy too with different things, but I was wondering where you have been. I have been here a few times looking for you'.

'I am sorry about that, Jack', she said. Jack had with him a cool box, and he opened the lid.

'Do you want to have a drink of wine? I have a couple of bottles of wine here'.

'Yes, please. I will have a small one. I have not had a drink for a long time. I do not suppose one will hurt me'.

With that, Jack poured out a small glass for her and handed it to Maria.

'Thank you, Jack', she replied.

They started to chat about different things. She told him about her friend Jimmy, who had passed away.

'I am deeply sorry', he said. 'Such a shame when people you like pass away'.

They sat there for quite some time, and Maria had more than a few glasses of wine. She was feeling quite relaxed and in a good mood. The time was getting on.

'Jack, would you like to come to my flat and have a coffee?'

'That would be nice', he replied. So, with that, they packed up the chairs.

'You can leave your car where it is, Jack. I am near to here, where I live. We can walk to my flat'.

Eventually, they reached her flat.

'I will put the kettle on', replied Maria.

Jack could see how things were very tidy in her flat, and he was making himself quite comfortable and looking around at the photos. He could see the television star Timothy Daily. He got up and looked at the photo. He could see it was signed for her.

She came in with the coffee, nicely laid out with the milk on the side and a sugar container.

'I see you like Timothy Daily. You've got a signed photo from him'.

'Yes', she said. 'He sent it to me'.

Maria did not tell him that she had a date with him. She did not think he would be interested.

'Take a seat, Jack'.

He sat on the sofa. Suddenly, Jack put his arm around her and said, 'I am so glad that we have met again'.

By this time, she was wondering what she could do to dissuade Jack from getting too close to her. She didn't mind, because it was nice to be made a fuss of; something that she had been lacking in her life. He turned round to her.

59

'I love being with you', he said, and with that, he kissed her passionately on the lips.

She responded by putting her arms around him and she whispered, 'I am so glad we are good friends, Jack'.

He started to unzip her cardigan, and he slipped it down to her back.

'No', said Maria. 'Please', she said in a passionate way.

He took no notice and suddenly started unzipping her blouse. His hand went inside her blouse. He was very gentle, and his hand was very warm, and she felt very secure. Suddenly, she started to undo the buttons on his shirt.

'Jack...'

He put his hand on Maria's leg. She could not resist his touches. They kissed again passionately. She slipped his shirt over his shoulders, and she could see his body. Jack was well developed. Eventually, they were both completely naked.

Gently, he lifted her down onto the carpet, kissing her gently on her breasts. They made love there and then.

Maria couldn't understand how she had let him go so far. Was it the drink that made her give in to him? She knew she didn't love him. She started to get dressed. While she was doing that, she was hoping that Jack would go and leave her on her own. She thought to herself that she loved her television star, Eddie.

Quickly, Jack got dressed. He didn't talk. He just said he would see her soon and left the flat.

Maria was so surprised that he left so quickly. She was taken aback. She thought to herself, 'I have been so stupid'.

Maria felt ashamed that she had let this happen to her. 'What now?' she thought to herself. 'How am I going to live with this?'

She sat down on the sofa and started to cry. She thought she had betrayed Eddie. She closed her eyes and fell asleep.

Chapter 16
Confession

Maria couldn't seem to sleep. She got off the settee and went to her bed. She tossed and turned all night long, thinking about what had happened with Jack. Was it Jack's plan to get her drunk so she would be an easy target for him to make love to her? She knew she should not have let him take advantage of her.

According to her religion, you shouldn't be having sex before marriage, and this extensively played on her mind. She had committed a mortal sin. She telephoned the Care Home manager and said she had an appointment and would be a little late. She decided to go to the local church's early Mass and see if she could speak to the priest after the service to ask for confession.

Father Jeremy was the parish priest of her local church. He was in his late sixties and had been at the church for twenty years. He had got to know Maria over time, and they used to talk quite often. She had helped at the church on several occasions.

She could not take communion because she knew she had committed a mortal sin. She had to be in a state of grace before receiving communion from Father Jeremy. When Mass finished, she managed to speak to him and explained what had happened.

He agreed to hear her confession and told her, 'Go into the confessional. I will get ready to hear your confession'.

She confessed to the priest. After that, she felt so much better.

Maria returned to work. She did not know whether she should tell Pauline what had happened. She decided not to tell her and resolved to put it all behind her. Still, she worried; should she tell Eddie when she met him in a week's time? It kept playing on her mind. She couldn't concentrate on her work. She was glad the episode in her life was over, but she still had to decide whether to be honest with Eddie and tell him about Jack.

She completed her rounds as best she could. All the patients on her list she managed to visit. After she finished work, she returned to her flat to watch her favourite programme, *Down in the Country*, which was coming on television. She decided she would watch that.

The programme this time was about Timothy Dailey and his affair with Ruth. He was in trouble because Ruth wanted to end the affair, and he didn't. Ruth said that if he did not accept it, she would report him.

At this point, Maria was quite disappointed. After the programme finished, she decided to retire to bed early.

Chapter 17
Date with Eddie

On Tuesday, Maria was preparing to meet Eddie the following day for their dinner date. She received a phone call from him asking if it was still all right for them to meet.

She said, 'Yes, that is fine'.

He replied that he would come to Ramsgate at 7 p.m. and then call her to take her out to dinner. She gave him her address, which he noted down.

The next day, she rushed home to get herself ready. Maria had already booked the restaurant with a table for two. She was quite nervous. She said to herself, 'I wonder what I should say to him'.

By the time she was ready, it was nearly 7 p.m. The doorbell rang. She answered it, and there was Eddie, standing there in a smart blue suit and tie. He looked very well turned out.

Maria had made an effort to look nice herself. He escorted her to his car, and they drove to the restaurant where the reserved table was.

They were shown to their table by the waiter, who asked, 'Would you like a drinks menu, sir?'

'Yes, please', replied Eddie.

He turned to Maria. 'What would you like to drink?'

64

She said, 'May I have a small bottle of wine, please? Any red wine they have will be OK'.

Eddie ordered a bottle of the very best red wine the restaurant had. They both looked over the menu and decided what to eat.

They both really enjoyed the meal. Eddie had ribeye steak with cheese on top, and Maria had salmon.

Maria wondered to herself whether she should tell Eddie that she had been with another man. How could she explain what had happened? She thought, *I will not tell him anything at this time. I'll just see how the evening goes.*

Eddie acted like a true gentleman, making a fuss about her and telling her all about his career. They also talked about the television programme *Down in the Country*, in which he was appearing. Maria was very interested and listened intently.

They stayed at the restaurant until about 10 p.m., then decided it was time to leave.

'I'll take you home', he said.

'OK', she replied.

She asked him if he would like a coffee before heading back on the long trip to London. The evening went very well. Around 11:30, after more conversation, he kissed Maria on the cheek, and then he kissed her gently on the lips.

She was so excited about the evening. They made another date for the following week.

He asked, 'Could you get a train to London to meet me? I'll take you to the theatre to see *The Phantom of the Opera*'.

'Thank you, that would be nice', she said.

They fixed a time and date for her to travel to London. He then walked to his car and kissed her goodbye. She waited for him to drive off.

She went to bed feeling very satisfied. All she could think about was Eddie, and how she must tell him what had happened with Jack. She wanted to be honest with him. She didn't want anything to go wrong with their relationship.

She said to herself, 'I don't think it would be a good idea to tell him that I had been unfaithful. Perhaps he wouldn't understand and wouldn't want anything more to do with me'.

She made up her mind that she would tell her friend Pauline tomorrow morning, when she went to work, all about the date and how Eddie had been such a gentleman.

Chapter 18
Moving into a New Part of the Building

The building was ready. It had a separate entrance, and everywhere looked fresh and new. The builders had done a really good job converting the space into a separate care home. Although it retained the name *Southfield's Care Home*, the Mayor of Ramsgate had been invited to attend and cut the ribbon at the opening ceremony.

There were no patients there on the day of the ceremony. They were expected to arrive the following day to be welcomed to the care home. To start with, three patients were being sent by the NHS. The new building could accommodate forty patients in total.

Lots of new staff had been recruited. After the mayor gave a short speech, the ribbon was cut and the building was officially opened. A plaque would be placed on the wall at the entrance, displaying the date and the name of the mayor who had opened it. A small buffet was arranged for the staff and invited guests. When the opening ceremony ended, Maria and the rest of the staff got to work preparing the care home for the patients.

The next day, Maria started early. She wanted to personally welcome the new patients as they arrived by ambulance, one at a time. At 10 a.m., the first patient arrived, right on time. The driver showed the lady into the reception and asked her to sit down.

Maria's first task was to show Charlotte Fox round the centre. Her medical records had already been sent over electronically, so the staff knew what to expect. Charlotte was shown to her room, and she looked quite surprised and reassured. The room had brand new furnishings, a television, and a comfortable chair.

Maria told her, 'I'll be coming by shortly to take your blood pressure and temperature—just the usual checks we do with everyone'.

Charlotte nodded, but Maria could see how nervous she was. She looked very withdrawn and was shaking slightly.

Maria asked gently, 'Are you OK, Charlotte?'

Charlotte answered quietly, 'Yes'.

It was difficult to get any sort of conversation from her.

Maria said to one of the care assistants, 'I think we'll need to be very patient with Charlotte. She seems to have a lot of problems'.

Maria had already reviewed her medication and was hopeful she would quickly improve and be discharged. She explained the meal times and how to get drinks during the day. Charlotte had been living on her own and didn't have much support from her family.

Care Assistant Ruth came to see her and asked, 'Would you like tea or coffee and a small snack, Charlotte?'

Charlotte replied, 'Yes, please. I've not managed to have any breakfast'.

Ruth said, 'No problem. I'll bring you a sandwich'.

Charlotte felt reassured by the treatment she was receiving.

At noon, the second patient arrived by ambulance from the hospital. Her name was Sarah Little. The third lady, Jacqueline Spence, arrived the following day. Both were made to feel very welcome. Ruth made sure they had tea or coffee, and each of them received a routine check-up.

Maria told them, 'The doctor will come to speak with you at 4 p.m.'.

After finishing their drinks, the ladies were shown to their rooms. They both felt pleased that they were going to be properly cared for.

Jacqueline Spence was in her late twenties and suffered from anxiety and depression. Sarah's case was different, but she also struggled with her mental health.

Maria was very satisfied with how the day had gone. The staff had been extremely helpful.

She said to herself, 'This is going to be a wonderful job. I'm really going to enjoy this position, and it'll be a new experience for me—looking after people suffering from mental illnesses'.

Maria knew that mental illness carried a certain stigma, and it was part of her role to help end that stigma, and to support people in living full and active lives with the appropriate treatment.

All the patients would be supported by Mrs Johnson, a social worker who would help them cope with future needs, such as housing, jobs, and advice.

Most of the patients were heavy smokers, something quite common in mental health hospitals. A specially-designated smoking area had been set up for them. Maria knew she couldn't stop them from smoking. During her training, she had learned about the effect cigarettes had on some medications and how smoking helped some patients stay calm and relaxed.

Charlotte Fox, in particular, was a very heavy smoker. She would become extremely anxious and begin shaking if she couldn't have a cigarette.

The psychiatrist was well aware of the issue. Nicotine addiction was powerful, and it wasn't something easily controlled in patients. It was treated much like a drug. Staff were instructed to be very careful about how cigarettes were disposed of, and no patients were allowed to smoke in their rooms. That rule was strictly enforced.

Maria had personally put this policy in place. The patients knew about it and respected the rule.

This NHS trial aimed to explore whether this approach could improve mental health recovery, and Maria was proud to be part of it.

Chapter 19
Bad News

The telephone rang. Ben Hutchinson answered, 'Southfield's Care Home'.

A woman spoke in a quiet tone. 'I'm calling about my daughter, Pauline Watson. I have some sad news: she was killed in a car accident yesterday. I thought I should let you know. I can't speak much now because I'm terribly upset. I'll give you more information later when I receive it'.

Ben didn't know what to say. He was so shocked that he simply replied, 'Thanks for letting me know. I'll pass on your message'.

Ben could not believe what he had just heard. He sat there in silence.

I wonder how that happened, he said to himself.

Pauline had been a very good nurse at the Care Home and was truly respected. He knew she lived with her elderly parents, and her father had suffered several strokes. Pauline used to look after him as much as she could, especially on her days off.

From the beginning, she had been devoted to her job, starting at Southfield's when it first opened. Over the years, she had built up quite a rapport with the residents. She always had time to talk to them, and they trusted her with their concerns.

She was best friends with Maria. They had been close for the past four years and often shared their worries with each other. It was rare to see them apart during breaks.

Pauline had been preparing to take her exam to become an SRN, which would have given her more responsibility and experience in looking after the residents. As an SEN, there were some limitations on what she could do. She had only just passed her driving test two months ago.

Ben wondered, *Could that have had anything to do with the accident?*

Straight away, he telephoned Maria.

'Can you come see me, please? I need to have a word with you. Something has happened that I must tell you about'.

Ten minutes later, Maria arrived at Ben's office.

'Please sit down, Maria. I have some really bad news I must share with you. Nurse Pauline has been tragically killed in a car accident'.

At first, Maria couldn't believe what she was hearing. She was so upset she had to go home; she couldn't continue her shift.

The next day, Maria returned to the Care Home. As soon as she entered the main building, she went to speak to some of the residents to break the sad news. Many were visibly upset, and tears filled several eyes.

Maria did her best to comfort them. She asked Care Assistant Ruth to make some cups of coffee. Then she decided to hold a meeting with the staff to inform them properly about the situation.

Maria didn't know the exact cause of death, only that it had been a car accident. She explained to the staff what had happened. Most were horrified to hear such tragic news.

Some asked questions Maria couldn't answer. She did her best to respond but couldn't hold back the tears.

I've lost my best friend, she thought to herself. *I'll never forget her*.

She knew she needed to visit Pauline's parents. *They must be devastated*, she thought.

The following morning, Maria rang Pauline's mother to ask if she could come round to see them. She was relieved when Pauline's mother said, 'Yes, please come around first thing in the morning'.

Maria phoned Ben to let him know she would be away for a few hours. He agreed.

When she arrived at the house, she paused at the door, hesitating. *What shall I say?* she wondered. Finally, she gathered her courage and rang the doorbell.

Pauline's mother answered straight away. They embraced, and both broke into tears.

'Can you tell me what happened?' Maria asked gently.

Her mother took a deep breath and said, 'There's going to be an investigation. Someone was driving in the wrong direction on the wrong side of the road. It was a head-on collision. Pauline was killed instantly'.

Pauline's father was sitting quietly in the living room.

'I don't think he fully realises what's happened', said Mrs Watson.

Maria went into the kitchen and made them both some coffee.

'Maria', Pauline's mother said, 'I know you were her best friend. She relied on you a lot for advice. When they release her body, would you kindly help me plan the arrangements? I don't think I'll have the strength to do it'.

Maria replied, 'Yes, of course. That's no problem. Just let me know when. I'll help you'.

After a while, Maria left to go back to work. She didn't know how she would cope without Pauline. The thought of not having her there to talk to was unbearable.

Chapter 20
Going to the Theatre

Maria decided she would take three days' holiday, which she was due. She left early to catch a taxi to the railway station. She arrived in London in mid-morning. She thought to herself it would be better if she could have a look around London and stop for lunch. Pauline was on her mind. As soon as she got back to Ramsgate, she was going to arrange the funeral, which she had promised Pauline's parents.

She thought to herself how much London had changed. She was looking forward to going and seeing the show *Phantom of the Opera*. She had heard a lot about it, and she had read in the local papers regarding the show.

She was due to meet Eddie at 6:00 p.m., so she thought that if she phoned him at 5:00 p.m. and told him she was in London, that would be her plan. She thought to herself, she might as well have a trip around London.

She hadn't been to London for a long time, and she would like to see some of the sights. She caught the Underground and went to Baker Street, and then made her way to Madame Tussauds. She spent an hour and a half there. She also visited the Chamber of Horrors, but she didn't stay in there long. She couldn't stand looking at some of the murderers who had been hanged, including Christie, Hanratty and Haigh, the Acid Bath Murderer.

When she left, she walked down Baker Street, trying to find the house that Sherlock Holmes lived in, but she realised it was just a story and there wasn't an actual house that took place in the novels. She then decided she would go to Tower Hill and have a walk around the Tower of London. She did have an affinity with Anne Boleyn because she was interested in history, and she thought to herself, *I don't know why. That lady was innocent in the past. I have lighted a candle in her memory, and Henry was not a genuinely nice man. He had lots of people executed for no reason at all.*

Maria managed to go into St George's Chapel and have a look at the wonderful church with all the pictures of the kings and queens, where some of the kings and queens were buried. She did go on to the church in the White Tower and sat there for ten minutes, and realised that the time was getting late, so she had to go and meet Eddie.

Five o'clock soon came around, and it was now time for her to contact Eddie. She phoned.

'Hello, it is me', she said.

When he answered, he said, 'Hello, Maria. I will come and meet you. Do you know where you are?'

'Yes, I am outside George's Restaurant in Tower Hill. I will have a coffee; I am waiting for you'.

Eddie arrived on time. 'I have booked a table so we can have a meal before we go to the show', he said.

'That would be nice', Maria answered.

He took her to a posh restaurant. After they finished their meal, it was time for them to go to the show. They arrived half an hour before the show started. There were lots of people sitting in the entrance. Some of the staff in the theatre were going round selling programmes and different replicas from the show.

Eddie said to Maria, 'Would you like a programme?'

'Yes, please', answered Maria.

Eddie purchased two coffees while they were waiting for the show to start. The show started on time at 7:30. During the performance, Eddie held Maria's hand. She squeezed his hand slightly, and they both looked at each other. She knew at this time that she was about to go into a relationship with him.

The show finished. Eddie suggested they go back to his flat in Ealing for coffee and drinks. She was incredibly pleased. It was quite a long drive from the West End to Ealing, but eventually they came to his flat.

'Come in', he said.

He opened the door, and she could see this beautiful flat with beautiful furniture. Obviously, you could see he was a successful actor.

Before Maria set off for London, she had booked a bed and breakfast. She knew it would be too late for her to travel back to Ramsgate. She asked Eddie if he could run her to the hotel, which she had booked.

He replied, 'Do not worry about that. You can stay at my flat overnight. I have a spare room which you can have'.

'Thank you, Eddie', she replied. 'That's kind of you'.

'I was thinking of that all the time. I am sorry, I should have told you. You do not want to spend the money on bed and breakfast. You can stay here'.

Eddie said, 'Would you like a drink? I can make you a coffee if you would like. Would you like a gin and tonic?'

At first, Maria did not know what to say. She thought to herself, *Now I'm here, I might as well make the most of it*, so she accepted the gin, tonic and the coffee.

Eddie went to his drinks cabinet and mixed up the drinks, and then he put the kettle on to make coffee.

'I will put some music on', he said.

He had a vinyl record player, and he put on Nat King Cole. The music started to play, and they started to have their drinks and sip their coffee. Suddenly, he said to her, 'Would you care to dance with me?'

She accepted his invitation. They started to dance. Suddenly, after a little while, Eddie put his arms round Maria. He kissed her on the side of her face.

'Maria', he said, 'I loved you from the first time I met you. I knew I was in love with you'.

She was taken aback. She did not know how to answer. She just held him in her arms and gently whispered at the side of his face, 'Eddie, I love you, Eddie', in an incredibly soft voice.

The music of Nat King Cole was very quiet. Nat started to sing *Mona Lisa*. They held each other in their arms.

Eddie then started to unbutton her top from the front of her blouse. He unfastened the zip on her skirt. She didn't stop him. She just closed her eyes. He took the zip down slowly. The skirt fell to the floor. Then he slid her blouse down her back gently with each hand and slid it down her side. The dress also fell to the floor.

Maria could not believe what was happening to her. She could not stop him. He unclipped her bra and moved it off her shoulders. He then dropped it onto the floor.

Maria, by this time, was getting more excited. He took off her panties, and she was completely naked. He stretched his arms and held her away from him. He looked at her and smiled. Maria was feeling relaxed.

'Eddie, I should not be doing this', she said to Eddie in her soft voice.

Again, Eddie said to Maria, 'I love you, darling, and I would never do anything to hurt you. I have never felt this way about any other woman'.

When he said that, Maria just gave in to him. Eddie took off his shirt and the rest of his clothes. They were both naked, standing with each other. He held Maria's hands outstretched and looked at her.

He said, 'Maria, I love you', then took her towards the bed, still kissing her passionately. They made love, and they held each other close together and kissed passionately.

Maria knew that she loved him. She could not help herself. They lay in each other's arms close together. After a little while, he kissed her on the lips and made love to her a second time. Maria was so contented. She was with her heart's desire, and they both decided that they would go to sleep.

In the morning, Maria woke before Eddie. Maria quickly got dressed. Maria decided that she would make tea before he awoke. After they had their tea, they had breakfast together. After they finished their breakfast, Maria had to leave early to catch the train back to Ramsgate.

Eddie drove her to the train station. Before she got out of the car, he kissed her passionately and said, 'I will be in touch'. He said to her that he would write her some letters and that they would meet again soon.

Maria caught the 10:00 train to take her back to Ramsgate. She closed her eyes on the train and started to think about him. She could not think of anything else but Eddie. The only thing she could not do was tell her friend Pauline about her trip to London. She was extremely disappointed about this.

I miss Pauline so much, she commented to herself.

Chapter 21
Pauline Watson

Maria returned home. She had one day of her holiday left, so she decided she would visit Pauline's parents and talk about the funeral arrangements. She telephoned her mother.

'Catherine, is it OK if I can see you and talk about the funeral?'

'Yes, that's fine, Maria'.

Maria arrived in the morning and was greeted by Pauline's mother. They had a little cuddle and a quiet weep.

'Have the police released her yet?' Maria asked.

'Yes', she answered. 'So I can contact the undertaker to bring her from the hospital'.

'Thank you', Maria replied.

All the arrangements were made. Catherine contacted the local priest who agreed to conduct the service. Pauline was not a Catholic, but it didn't matter. The priest said he would still carry out the ceremony.

Pauline wasn't deeply religious, unlike Maria, but she did believe in God and was a very good person. She had qualified as a State Enrolled Nurse seven years ago and had carried out her training in London at one of the big teaching hospitals. She studied a two-year course in various types of nursing. After passing her

83

exams, she worked at the hospital where Maria was employed – the local general hospital in Ramsgate.

Pauline had many interests in her life. She was very involved in amateur dramatics and used to help when her theatre company put on shows. Sometimes she even performed in them. She took on several parts and was a very good singer. In one of the shows where she starred as the lead singer, she received excellent reviews.

She also loved classical music and often attended the local theatre to hear orchestras play different classical pieces. She never had a regular boyfriend. Years ago, she was in a romantic relationship with a colleague from the repertory theatre, but it didn't last.

Pauline loved going to the theatre and watching plays that interested her. She had also been appointed as Deputy Nurse to Maria. She was thrilled when she got the job and was incredibly happy with the work she was doing.

Maria made some enquiries to find out what had happened to the person who drove into Pauline's car and caused the accident. He had been charged with manslaughter and was awaiting trial. He intended to plead not guilty.

Maria decided that when the court case took place, she would attend and find out if he would be found guilty. Pauline's parents would not go to court due to their health issues. Maria assured them not to worry; she would keep them informed.

The funeral took place at Maria's church. Several members of staff from the care home attended, along with Pauline's parents and people from the operatic society, who sat in the front row. Maria gave the eulogy. She said that Pauline was her best friend, a dedicated nurse, and someone loved by everyone who met her. She added that Pauline would be greatly missed, especially by her and her parents.

The service was conducted by the priest. He told the congregation that Pauline would definitely meet her parents in heaven one day. After the service ended, Pauline was taken to the local cemetery, where she was laid to rest. Everyone was upset; she was a favourite Care Home nurse.

After the burial, most of those who attended the funeral went to a local venue for the wake. It was a quiet time, where people simply reflected on Pauline's life.

Maria turned to Ben, her manager, and said, 'I hope the person who drove into her car gets what he deserves'.

Maria returned to her flat after the funeral. As she opened the door, she picked up a letter that looked very important. It read: *Private and Confidential – for the addressee only.*

She sat down, looked at the envelope, and wondered what it was all about. She had no idea what to expect.

Chapter 22
The Will

Maria received a letter from the solicitors:

Dear Miss Giovanna,

We are writing to you to inform you that we have something to your advantage. As you know, the late Jimmy West has announced that you have been featured in his will. We would like to invite you to come into the office at your convenience.

If you can telephone the office and let us know when you will be coming, that would be much appreciated. On your arrival at the office, can you please ask for Patrick Barrett.

Yours faithfully,
Patrick Barrett
Solicitor

Maria was surprised to receive the letter and started to wonder what it was all about. Suddenly, she had an idea – it could be to do with Jimmy, her ex-patient at Southfields Care Home. This brought back memories of Jimmy. She hadn't wanted to be featured in his will, but she thought it was truly kind of him to think about her.

She went to see Ben, her manager, and told him she had received a letter from the solicitor's office.

He told her, 'You should phone the solicitor and find out what it's all about in Jimmy's will'.

Ben suggested, 'If you want me to, I could come with you to support you at this time'.

Maria said, 'It's OK. I'd better go on my own, that's what Jimmy would have wanted'.

She immediately telephoned the solicitor and asked for Mr Barrett. She booked an appointment to see him. When she arrived, she was met by the receptionist, who told her to take a seat while she informed Mr Barrett that Maria had arrived.

After a short while, Mr Barrett came out to where she was sitting and greeted her.

'Thank you for coming to see me', he said. 'Come on in, Miss Giovanna. Please take a seat'.

Maria, a little nervously, sat down. He stepped out to speak with the receptionist.

'Can you bring me the Jimmy West file?'

Miss Jenkins, the receptionist, handed the file to Mr Barrett. She then asked Maria, 'Would you like tea or coffee?'

'No, I'm fine', replied Maria.

She was in no mood to drink tea or coffee. She was just waiting to hear what was going to be said.

'I've just heard from the probate office. It took a few weeks for this to be completed, but it has just been granted', said the solicitor. 'I have Jimmy's will. If you're ready, I will read you the contents. I'll start by saying that you are the main beneficiary in Jimmy's will'.

She could not believe what he was saying. She sat in the chair with her hands clenched and a stern look on her face, as she had not taken much notice of what Jimmy had once said to her.

Maria replied to Mr Barrett, 'Jimmy told me he was going to leave me something in his will and that he would look after me. I didn't know to what extent he meant, so I didn't pay much attention to it'.

The solicitor continued, 'I must admit, you have now become a very wealthy woman. I'll read you the full contents of the will'.

'The first thing stated in the will is that he has left £10,000 to Southfields Care Home and has asked that it be used for the benefit of the residents. He has also stated, "I would like to leave £3,000 to any charity Nurse Maria suggests for elderly people that would benefit them in their old age".'

'And to Maria Giovanna, I leave my property, possessions, and my house at the said address. The keys to the house will be handed to Maria Giovanna from the solicitors on the reading of this will'.

'I also leave one and a half million pounds to Maria, as custodian of my estate and said artefacts, in gratitude to her for the wonderful support she gave me during my stay at Southfields Care Home. During this time of my illness, Nurse Maria looked after me with great passion, and I was so grateful to her. This is my last will and testament, witnessed by the undersigned'.

She could not believe what was happening. She was shaking and perspiring slightly. She was speechless and couldn't believe what she had heard. The solicitor came over and shook her hand. He handed her the keys to the house she had been left in the will.

'I'm afraid there will be some inheritance tax to pay from the legacy you've received, but we will sort that out for you', he said.

'You should receive the money in your bank account in the near future. Please leave your bank details with our secretary, and we'll make the necessary arrangements. We can now also give you the artefacts he's left you. The medals he has left are worth quite a bit of money. One of the medals is very valuable—the Victoria Cross, with the citation he received in World War II. We've had this medal valued for you for insurance purposes, and it is worth £138,000. We suggest you get this medal insured as soon as possible. If you decide to keep it, that's entirely your decision. If you choose to sell it and need advice, you can always contact our office'.

Maria took a deep breath. He handed her the medals, wished her all the best, and bid her farewell.

She then left and returned to her apartment to prepare for work at the care home the following day.

When she got back to her flat, she just could not believe what had taken place at the solicitor's office.

What will I do with all that money? she said to herself.

She sat down, thinking about Jimmy and how kind he was to have considered her in his will. She never thought she had helped him that much. She made herself a cup of coffee because she was still shaking with excitement. Then she went to the cupboard and poured herself a glass of wine to steady her nerves.

'How will I sleep?' she said out loud.

She couldn't even watch her favourite programme, although she had decided she would never watch it again. But she couldn't resist the temptation and ended up watching it anyway.

As the time got late, she decided she would go to bed and see if she could sleep. The excitement had got to her. She closed her eyes, and after a little while, she fell asleep.

Chapter 23
Working Hard

Maria started the next day at work. She had to go in to see Ben Hutchinson, the manager, about her legacy. She also told him that Jimmy had left £10,000 to be used for the benefit of the patients. He was so pleased that they were going to receive this money. It would certainly help to equip the living room—it would be a nice recreation area for them with new carpets and comfortable chairs, so the clients could sit and watch television.

She did not tell Ben how much money she had personally been left. However, she did mention the Victoria Cross medal she had received from Jimmy. He was intrigued.

'I want to hear all about the meeting with the solicitor', he said.

She told him that she wasn't sure what to do with the medal yet, as she hadn't decided. She also mentioned that the insurance premium would be high due to the medal's value.

'I'll sort this out later', she said.

Ben commented, 'Collectors would be especially interested in it, particularly as it comes with a citation. You should go to one of the auction houses and get their opinion on the value, whether you plan to sell it or not.

She listened to what he had to say and thought to herself that he was being very kind in offering his advice. She decided that the next time she returned to London, she would visit Christie's Auction House and see if they would be interested in helping her sell it.

A new charge nurse was going to start the following day to replace Maria, who was now working in the annexe for mental patients from the National Health Service. The new nurse had lots of experience looking after patients, and she was qualified to prescribe different medications for them.

Maria was looking forward to meeting Nurse Rita Edwards. She was sure she was going to fit in very well.

Ben asked Maria, 'Could you show Rita around the care home and introduce her to some of the patients?'

She was very happy to do this.

The next day, Maria showed Rita all around the care home. She introduced her to most of the elderly people. They went in to see Mr and Mrs Rogers, who were in separate rooms. Mr Rogers was not at all well and was bedridden. Maria told Rita all about Mr Rogers, how he was very eccentric and had some funny stories to tell.

Mrs Rogers was in better health, although she had difficulty walking due to an arthritic hip. She was waiting for surgery.

Maria returned to her department to do her rounds and make sure the patients she was looking after were well settled into their new routine. There were now 15 patients in her care, all sent by the NHS. The annexe had the capacity to take 25 more. All the rooms were ready for the patients.

Patients were allowed to come and go if they wanted, and they could go shopping accompanied by a member of staff.

Maria was very popular with the patients, and they all got on well with her. After a little time, some of the patients were discharged and returned home, where they would be monitored by a Mental Health Nurse. The annexe was performing well under Maria's leadership, and the first set of reviews was very encouraging.

Maria went to see Charlotte Fox. She had to make sure that Charlotte had taken her medication, as she was under special observation. When Maria entered her room, there was no sign of her. Maria then went to the community room to see if she could find her there, but there was no sign of her either. She asked one of the Care Assistants to have a look around the annex to try and find Charlotte and tell her she had to take her medication.

After a little while, there was still no sign of her.

Maria returned to Charlotte's room just in case she had doubled back. She noticed that her dressing gown was missing. *She must have put it on and just wandered off somewhere*, Maria thought.

She went outside and asked James, the gardener, if he had seen Charlotte.

'She was smoking, sitting on the bench. I didn't pay any attention to her, thought it was quite normal', he replied.

Maria came to the conclusion that Charlotte had wandered off. She immediately telephoned the police and informed them that one of her patients was missing from the annexe. Straight away, an alert went out, and eventually, the police arrived at the care home to get further details.

Maria told the police that Charlotte was a very vulnerable person. Some care assistants walked around the local area to look for her, but when they returned, they told Maria there was still no sign of her. Maria began to grow increasingly worried about her condition. The police issued an all-station alert. Eventually, a police helicopter was seen hovering above the care home and the surrounding area.

A member of the public had found Charlotte wandering around and assumed she was from Southfields Care Home. They telephoned the police to report her. The police picked her up and brought her back to the care home.

Maria took her into her room and called the doctor. He took her blood pressure and said, 'She's fine; just a little confused'.

'Charlotte, why did you wander off?' Maria asked.

Charlotte replied, 'I don't like it here anymore. I want to go home'.

Maria explained, 'Charlotte, we're here to look after you and make sure you get better. When that happens, you *can* go home. Just be patient, and if you need anything, let us know – we'll help you'.

Charlotte was reassured by Maria's words.

Maria immediately called a meeting with the senior care staff to try to find out how Charlotte had managed to wander off without anyone seeing her. It was then decided they would install an intercom system on the front door with a combination lock. Exit would only be possible with a special code.

Maria was satisfied that this would help the situation and prevent patients from wandering off again.

After her shift, Maria returned home to find a letter waiting for her. Looking at the envelope, she could tell it was from Eddie.

My Darling Maria,

I just wanted to let you know that I'm doing OK and I've been very busy rehearsing and starring in the soap opera. I hope we can meet very soon. I'm planning to come to Ramsgate – perhaps I could stay for a couple of days, if you have room to put me up in your flat.

I've missed you, and I'm looking forward to seeing you very soon. I hope you've missed me.

I think about you all the time—about our lovely time together—and I was sorry that you had to leave to go back to Ramsgate. I certainly do understand that your work is very important to you. That's why I'm coming to be with you shortly. As soon as I have a date, I'll let you know.

I hope this letter finds you in good health and that you're enjoying your job looking after those lovely patients you told me about.

I've been offered several parts by directors for adverts that will be shown on national television. I'll let you know when I'll appear in them so you can look out for me.

I must go now, my darling, as they're waiting for me at the studio for rehearsals.

All my love,

Eddie

XX

Maria answered Eddie's letter straight away.

My Dearest Eddie,

This is just a short letter to thank you for your beautiful message. I've read it over and over again.

Of course, you can come and stay as before; telephone me and let me know when you're coming. I'm looking forward to seeing you soon.

At the moment, I'm very busy trying to sort out a few things, so that's why I'm keeping this letter short.

I've had this photo taken for you, which I will enclose.

Maria

Later, Pauline's mother telephoned Maria and told her that Brian Ayres was appearing in court today. He had changed his plea to guilty and would be sentenced. She had been notified by her daughter's solicitor and asked Maria if she could go and find out what happened to the man.

Maria got the time of the hearing from the court. It was at 10:00 a.m.

She managed to get time off work and arrived at the court just before the case began. The judge entered the courtroom, followed by the defendant, who had been on bail. He was only twenty-seven years old and smartly dressed.

The judge opened the case and said to him, 'I understand you've pleaded guilty to the charge of manslaughter, and I will accept that.

97

It just leaves me to say, you drove your car without due attention and, sadly, Miss Watson was killed instantly because you drove into her car, not paying attention. Miss Watson was a working nurse who had a bright future ahead of her. I understand that you have pleaded guilty, and I will take that into consideration. Therefore, I sentence you to three years' imprisonment, ban you from driving for ten years, and fine you £2,000 for costs'.

'Please, sir, may I say something?'

'In this case, I will allow you to speak', the judge said.

'I am sincerely sorry for what happened. If I could bring this lady back, I would', the young man said quietly.

The judge replied, 'Take him down'.

Maria shook her head and was quite shocked at the short sentence he had been given. She left the court and went straight round to see Pauline's parents.

'I was very shocked at the result', Maria told them, and explained what had happened.

Afterwards, Maria left and returned to the care home. When she finished work, she decided she would write another letter to Eddie.

Chapter 24
Eddie

Maria and Eddie's relationship blossomed. Eddie would come to see Maria on a regular basis, and they would go out for dinner. Their relationship deepened, and they both fell deeply in love.

On her last trip to London, Maria went to the auction house to make enquiries about the Victoria Cross medal. She was told that the record for a medal of that kind was over £100,000. With the citation, the auctioneer said it could be worth even more.

Maria hadn't yet decided whether to sell the medal. She didn't need the money. She told herself that she would think about it. Jimmy had left her very comfortable. She was thinking, in the long run, that she and Eddie might get married and buy a house together. They were looking at a house in Broadstairs, next to Ramsgate. She did think about the insurance for the medal, so the next time she was in London, she planned to sell the medal and put it up for auction.

Maria was back at work in the annexe, looking after people with certain mental health problems. During her tea break in the restroom, one of the mental health nurses said to her, 'Have you heard the news about your actor friend? He's been dropped from the TV programme *Down in the Country*'.

She couldn't believe what she was hearing. She asked her colleague, 'Why is he leaving the programme?'

'He's been dropped. They're going to kill him off', she replied.

Maria was shocked. She couldn't believe what she was being told. After her shift finished, she returned to her flat and immediately turned on the local news. They announced that Timothy Daly, the doctor in the long-running soap *Down in the Country*, was going to leave the show. In one of the episodes, his character would be killed off.

Maria was so upset. *Why hadn't Eddie told me he was going to be dropped from the show? What was the reason? Or was the television company just taking the programme in a different direction?*

The next day, she telephoned Eddie to find out if it was true.

She asked him, 'Are you leaving the show? And why didn't you tell me?'

Eddie replied, 'There's a different director taking over the show, and he wants to bring in new characters. That's what they do with long-running soaps—it keeps the public interested'.

The telephone conversation lasted a little while, and then they said goodbye to each other.

100

Maria decided she would write a letter to the television company to complain about dropping Timothy Daly from the show. Although she didn't think it would do any good, she wanted to make a point.

She sat down and started to write the letter.

Dear Producer

I am writing to let you know that I am a fan of your television programme *Down in the Country*. I am disappointed to find out that you are going to drop Timothy Daly from your show.

I urge you not to do this. He is one of the main characters, and if he goes, I will not watch the programme anymore – and I know many others who watch it will stop as well.

Yours sincerely
Maria Giovanna

Before going to London, Maria took the medal to the auctioneers. She posted the letter to the studio, wondering if she would receive a reply. At that stage, she didn't think so.

When she got to the auction house, she was met by Mr Tailor. He told her the auction would be held in seven days' time. They were going to place a reserve on the medal for £100,000, if she was happy with that.

She said, 'Yes, that would be nice. If I get £100,000 for it, I'll be happy'.

Mr Tailor, the auctioneer, told Maria that she could watch the auction via Zoom and see what sort of money it would bring. They informed her that they would take 20% commission. She was satisfied with that, thanked him, and wished him goodbye.

She went to see Eddie.

'Hello Maria. It's nice to see you – but I have some sad news. Please, Maria, sit down. Would you like tea, coffee, or perhaps something a little stronger?'

'No, I'm fine', she said, a little nervously. She didn't know what to expect.

'You're not going to be happy with me when I tell you this. I want to personally tell you that I've decided I'll be moving to Australia. I can't see any future in my acting career in this country. I've been in this show for a long time, and I think I'll be typecast and find it difficult to get other parts'.

He looked at her with a serious look in his eyes and continued, 'I really don't know how to say this, but I have to end it between you and me'.

There was a long pause. Neither of them could speak. Maria was completely shocked.

'Eddie, you know I love you, and I've given myself to you fully. Why are you doing this to me?'

Eddie stood speechless. He could see how hurt she was.

'All I can say, Maria, is that I'm sorry. I know you wouldn't be happy coming to Australia with me. Your career is your life. I understand you couldn't give it up for me'.

Maria didn't answer. She just looked at him. Suddenly, tears began to roll down her face.

'OK, Eddie, if that's what you want. I can't believe you're doing this to me. I thought we were going to get married and settle down. I thought we could adopt a couple of children. I've never been so happy in my life since I met you and you know that. I've supported you in your career. I've been patient, waiting for you while you were filming. I travelled to London many times just to see you. You know how much I love you, Eddie'.

He just stood there silently, unable to speak. At that moment, he didn't know what else to say but his mind was made up. He had to think about his future, and he knew it wasn't in this country.

'I'm sorry, Maria. I have to do this. Please understand that my career is very important to me. I'll never forget you or the happiness you gave me'.

Maria couldn't help herself. She stormed out of the flat and caught the train straight back to Ramsgate.

On the train, tears were rolling down her face. She couldn't stop crying. She just couldn't believe that Eddie would do this to her.

How selfish of him, she thought.

A lady sitting opposite her came over and said, 'Are you OK, dear? Is something the matter?'

Maria answered, 'Thank you, you're very kind. I'm just upset. My boyfriend has just dumped me. I'll be OK, and thank you for your concern'.

Chapter 25
Upset

Maria returned to her flat. She opened the door and fell straight onto the bed, and the tears came flooding down her face again. She could not think of anything else but being with Eddie. She lay on the bed for the next hour and decided she would write a letter to him, asking if he truly meant what he said. She couldn't understand how the relationship they had could come to an end.

She was about to write the letter, but then she decided it would not be a good idea. If he had made up his mind and was really going to Australia, then she would have to accept it. All her plans had gone out the window. She wanted to marry him and settle down to a nice life. Now, it was all ended.

She could not face going to work at the Care Home. After a few days, she telephoned the manager, Mr Ben Hutchinson, and told him about the situation, that she would need to stay off work for a little while. Her voice was shaking, and he could hear that she was crying.

'Maria', he replied, 'I understand fully what you are going through. You must take off as much time as you need. You can return to work when you're feeling better. I hope things will sort themselves out, and we'll be happy to see you back again as your old self'.

She could not think of anything else. It was constantly on her mind, and she began to feel it was her fault, that she couldn't hold a relationship, and she started to lose confidence in herself. She couldn't eat or manage anything around the flat.

A few days later, there was a knock on the door. She managed to get up and open it. Ben Hutchinson was standing there. She was quite surprised.

She invited him in.

'How are you getting on?' he asked.

'I'm not feeling too well. I'm still terribly upset about what has happened to me'.

'Don't worry', he said. 'I'll make sure that you'll be OK. If you want me to. I'll come back in a few days' time to see how you are'.

'That's kind of you, Ben'.

She was genuinely surprised that he had visited her. She had never realised that he cared about her.

After he left, Maria sat down to watch the television programme that Eddie had appeared in. She wanted to watch the last episode he had recorded. She never wanted to see that show again, but she felt she had to find out how they were going to drop him from it.

They certainly did kill him off. Two men involved in drugs confronted him, and when he tried to fight them, they shot him twice in the head.

Straight away, she had to turn off the television. She couldn't bear to watch it any longer.

A few days later, Ben Hutchinson came around to see her again. This time, he brought flowers and a box of chocolates.

He asked her, 'Do you want to return to work, or are you still not ready?'

Maria answered, 'Yes, I'll return on Monday, if that's OK with you'.

'Yes', he replied. 'That will be fine. I'll tell everyone that you're coming back to work'.

With that, he left the flowers and chocolates, said goodbye, and added, 'Maria, I'll see you on Monday'.

Chapter 26
Auction

Maria returned to work. She was still quite depressed, but she knew she had to carry out her duties. The first thing she had to do was catch up on all the paperwork and make sure the patients she was responsible for were being looked after.

A few more patients were arriving that day, so she had to make sure all the rooms were ready for them. After finishing her paperwork, she began to think about what she wanted to do with her future. She knew the annexe for the mental health patients meant a great deal to her, and she was determined to put in all the effort needed to ensure it received positive reviews.

A lot of things revolved around Maria. She visited most of the patients and went into the restaurant to speak with those who were having their tea, asking how they felt and whether they were happy and felt cared for. Most of the patients she spoke to seemed genuinely content. Maria was very pleased with their responses.

After a little while, Ben came to see her and asked, 'How are you keeping?'

She replied, 'Yes, I'm fine'.

'I'm thinking of holding a special party to celebrate my inheritance from Jimmy. What do you think?' Ben asked.

'I think that would be a clever idea. It would take your mind off things', Maria answered. 'In what format would you like the party to be, and where would you hold it?'

'I think I would book a hotel and use one of their big rooms. I could get a band and some caterers. I could invite some of my friends and acquaintances'.

Ben said, 'If you want any help organising the party, I could help you, if you want me to'.

Maria was quite surprised by how incredibly supportive he was.

'Thank you, Ben. That's truly kind of you. It would be great if you can help me find a hotel where I can hold the party'.

'OK, I'll start looking on the Internet and find a suitable venue. Then we can talk about organising a band and catering. Are you sure you don't mind me helping you?'

'Yes, that would be great', answered Maria.

Over the next couple of days, Maria felt much better and managed to catch up with all her paperwork.

Then she received a telephone call from the auction house.

'The auction will take place this Thursday. We've set up the Internet. The listing has gone all around the world. Do you have Zoom?'

'Yes', she answered. 'I can use it at my place of work. I'll be at work that day, so I'll watch it there'.

She was overly excited about the auction. Her thoughts turned to Jimmy, and she felt so grateful to him for leaving her the legacy and the house in his will. She also began thinking more seriously about the house he had left her and realised she would need to sort out his belongings and decide what to do with them.

On the day of the auction, she set up her computer and waited nervously for the Zoom stream to start. Suddenly, without warning, the auction began.

The auctioneer introduced the lot.

'This item is of special interest—the Victoria Cross awarded to Sergeant Jimmy West, a veteran of the Second World War, who risked his life rescuing three injured soldiers during the Battle of Dunkirk. With the medal is the citation he received for bravery. I'd like to start the bidding at £40,000. Do I have any bids in excess of this?'

The bidding began: £45,000, then £50,000, etc. The price continued to rise. Finally, the bidding ended at £120,000, and the medal was sold online.

Maria could not believe her good fortune. She was thrilled that the medal had been sold to a museum in the UK and would be placed on display for others to learn about Jimmy's bravery. That made her feel so much better. It helped her stop thinking about Eddie.

She had arranged a meeting with the staff at the annexe to discuss various matters concerning the patients and the upcoming inspection of the care home by the National Health Service.

She addressed the team.

'The inspectors will be coming to inspect the annexe. I have no worries. I'm very confident that everything that should be happening *is* happening. I want to thank all the staff for your dedication since we opened. I'm truly grateful to all of you, and I'm sure we'll receive a good report from the inspectors. Please keep up the good work; together, we will be successful'.

Chapter 27
House

Maria went to see Ben Hutchinson and mentioned that she was going to visit the house that had been left to her in Jimmy's will. It wasn't very far from the centre of Ramsgate. She asked Ben if he would like to accompany her, as she didn't fancy going into the house alone.

'Yes', he said. 'That's OK. When would you like to go?'

'I'll leave it up to you', she replied. 'When would you be free, Ben?'

'I'll go and check my diary and give you a date', he said. He left to check and returned shortly after. 'I can do tomorrow. I don't have much on'.

Maria thanked him. 'Do you have a time you'd prefer?'

'After we finish work, we could go then'.

When they left the care home the following day, they went straight to the house. Maria opened the front door, and they both stepped inside. It was clear from the atmosphere that a single person had lived there. Everything was a little untidy but still clean. There were many of Jimmy's belongings scattered around, and plenty of photos from his time in the army during World War II.

They went into the kitchen, which was full of old kitchen utensils and a microwave. Then they went upstairs. The bedrooms were all well furnished with cupboards, wardrobes, and beds. Though the house had charm, it was clear it needed work.

They stayed for about an hour.

Maria thanked Ben for coming with her. She explained that she hadn't yet decided what she would do with the contents or the house itself. She was considering putting it up for rent. The property needed a lot of work, but she had the money and could afford to renovate it into something beautiful.

Before they left the house, Ben looked at Maria, and she looked back at him. She felt a moment of quiet affection toward him. He had been so helpful and supportive during her most difficult times. As they were leaving, he reached out his hand. Their hands met, and he gently kissed her on the side of the cheek, then said goodbye and headed home.

Maria locked the house, made sure it was secure, and returned to her flat. She sat thinking about what to do with the house contents. The next day, she decided to get in touch with a house clearance company to arrange for everything to be removed.

She telephoned a company she found online and arranged for them to collect the keys and empty the house. She made it clear she didn't want any money for the items. She simply wanted the house cleared as soon as possible.

A few days later, the clearance company emptied everything, including Jimmy's clothes and other belongings. When they were finished, the house was completely bare.

Maria returned to the house a few days later with a builder. They walked through each room, and he began making a list of the necessary updates. She was planning to install a new kitchen, a new bathroom, central heating, and new windows. The property needed general repairs throughout. She also contacted a landscape gardener to design and renovate the garden.

The work would be carried out by the builder.

Maria hadn't yet decided whether she would rent the house out or sell it. She said she would make that decision in the future.

Chapter 28
Happy Times

Maria was overjoyed that Ben was helping her organise the party for her friends and acquaintances. Ben booked the hotel, which had a lovely ballroom, and arranged the catering. It was going to be expensive, but as far as Maria was concerned, money was no object. She was simply happy that the celebration was happening.

She invited many people from the care home. Most of the staff, except for a skeleton team who would remain to look after the residents. She also sent invitations to her relatives in Italy, and they agreed to come. Maria paid for their aeroplane tickets and hotel accommodation. It was all thanks to Jimmy, and she wanted to throw the party in his memory.

She received letters from her relatives confirming they were coming. The new owners of the vineyard were also planning to attend. Maria booked the flights and hotel rooms for seven relatives from Italy, who all checked into the hotel in Ramsgate.

She also hired a chauffeur-driven limousine to take them around Ramsgate and the surrounding areas. A day trip to London was arranged, including visits to Buckingham Palace and the Tower of London. Maria accompanied them on the outings and was delighted to see them looking so happy and enjoying themselves.

She said to her uncle Gino, 'Jimmy would have been proud of what I've done for our family'.

After the trip to London, they returned to their hotel in Ramsgate.

Two days later, the celebration in memory of Jimmy was due to take place. Ben was thrilled to see Maria relaxed and enjoying time with her family. She did not invite Eddie, who was now busy building his television career in Australia. She also didn't invite Jack. She still couldn't forgive herself for what had happened between them and had pushed those memories to the back of her mind.

Maria also invited people from the church, who kindly agreed to attend.

She donated £5,000 to the local drop-in centre to provide a small lunch for visitors on Thursdays. She wanted to help as many people as possible. Maria didn't feel right keeping all the money Jimmy had left her for herself. She was a good Christian woman and felt deeply that it should be used for good.

The celebration began. The band played, the catering was beautifully arranged, and everything ran smoothly. Everyone was enjoying themselves when Maria stopped the band and stepped up to the microphone to deliver a brief speech.

'My dear friends and colleagues, first of all, I'd like to thank you all for coming to this wonderful celebration. As most of you

117

know, Jimmy West, whom I looked after at the care home, was a very kind person. He made his feelings known to me and left me a vast amount of money.

I'd just like to take this opportunity for us to remember him. I ask you all now to stand quietly for a moment in his memory'.

They all stood in silence.

Towards the end of the party, the band played *The Last Waltz*. Ben came over to Maria and asked, 'May I have the last dance with you?'

Maria agreed, and they held each other closely. As they danced, Ben turned to her and said, 'The day I took you to the theatre, I knew I'd fallen in love with you'.

Maria took a deep breath. She realised she felt the same way. They kissed, and then the music stopped, signalling the end of the party. Everyone thanked Maria for hosting such a lovely evening.

Maria turned to Ben and asked, 'Would you like to come back to my flat for a last-minute drink?'

He smiled and said, 'I was hoping you'd say that'.

They left for her flat, which was now quite late. Maria made Ben a coffee, and they sat together, talking for a little while. She knew she could love Ben, not in the same way she had loved Eddie, but perhaps in a more lasting way.

He put his arm around her and kissed her gently on the lips. She closed her eyes, and they held each other. They looked into one another's eyes and realised they were both in love. Ben held her hand and led her to the bedroom. They lay in each other's arms, and eventually, they could not help themselves. They made love passionately.

Afterwards, Ben said, 'I would love to spend my life with you. I've always felt this way since the first time I took you to the theatre. I want to ask: Will you marry me? I know you've been through a lot, but I promise I'll look after you forever'.

Maria looked at him and said, 'I love you, and I'd be happy to be your wife'.

Five weeks later, they were married. They walked hand-in-hand along the beach, smiling, laughing, and kissing each other passionately.

The End

Postscript

The NHS gave Southfield Care Home a high rating. Maria and Ben had a long, happy marriage and adopted two children. Eddie had a successful career in Australia and remarried. Jack continued his work in the gym and eventually emigrated to America.

About the Author

Printed in Dunstable, United Kingdom

64791633R00077